"You again, Becky Latimore?"

There was no doubt about it, Jake Meadows was angry. Becky's fall had sent them both tumbling off the end of the pier—and into four feet of water. And now he was tangled in his fishing lines.

She listened to his mumbled curses, punctuated by a yelp of real pain. "You seem to have a fishhook stuck in your hand," she pointed out.

"Do I really? Now how in the world could that have happened?"

"You needn't be so sarcastic," she muttered. She could feel water in her eyes—from the fall into the lake, she told herself. She wouldn't be caught dead crying over this man!

"I'll be as sarcastic as I want," he roared back to her. "Every time you come near me, you're trouble. Did you hear that? Trouble!"

Emma Goldrick describes herself as a grandmother first and an author second. She was born and raised in Puerto Rico, where she met her husband, a career military man from Massachusetts. His postings took them all over the world, which often led to mishaps—such as the Christmas they arrived in Germany before their furniture. Emma uses the places she's been as backgrounds for her books, but just in case she runs short of settings, this prolific author and her husband are always making new travel plans.

Books by Emma Goldrick

HARLEQUIN ROMANCE

HARLEQUIN PRESENTS

Don't miss any of our special offers. Write to us at the following address for information on our newest releases.

Harlequin Reader Service
901 Fuhrmann Blvd., P.O. Box 1397, Buffalo, NY 14240
Canadian address: P.O. Box 603,
Fort Erie, Ont. L2A 5X3

Tempered by Fire
Emma Goldrick

Harlequin Books

TORONTO • NEW YORK • LONDON
AMSTERDAM • PARIS • SYDNEY • HAMBURG
STOCKHOLM • ATHENS • TOKYO • MILAN

Original hardcover edition published in 1986
by Mills & Boon Limited

ISBN 0-373-02846-6

Harlequin Romance first edition July 1987

CHAPTER ONE

THE axe thumped into the tree trunk he was using as a chopping block, and the handle trembled as he left it there. The hot morning sun burned his bare shoulders, now lubricated with perspiration, and it felt good. He flexed his arm muscles, laughing at the puny pile of split logs that surrounded him. But then why hurry? he asked himself. There was always this afternoon, or tomorrow, or next week, and the Lebanon was far away. He snatched up his wide-brimmed straw hat, collapsed on the thick grass, and tipped the hat over his eyes. It wasn't all bad, he told himself, for a man who had been ferried out to the hospital ship on a stretcher, and expected never to walk again.

One hand automatically plucked at a long grass stem. He chewed on it reflectively, shrugged his long thin body into a more comfortable position in the deep grass, and gradually drifted off to sleep.

It was the voices that brought him instantly awake. The soft voices. 'I *told* you there was somebody here!' It was a child's voice. He opened his eyes and gradually shifted his hat to one side. Three little stair-step children were standing holding hands. Fair curly hair, T-shirts, shorts, blue eyes. 'See?' the tallest of them repeated. 'I told you so!'

He sat up slowly, hardly believing his eyes. There was only one other house in this mountain cove besides his own. And in all the times he had been here, there had never been an inhabitant in that other, bigger, house.

'Hi,' he offered. He really had no idea how to deal with wandering children.

'Hi,' the tallest of them returned. 'I'm Faith. She's Hope. And——'

'I know,' he laughed. 'I don't believe it, but I know. Reading from left to right, Faith, Hope, and Charity?'

'Boy, have you got it wrong!' the middle one lisped at him. There was a gap in her teeth, and the words whistled.

He fumbled his hands around his knees and laughed again. 'So I'm wrong?'

'Of course,' the eldest returned. 'It's Faith, Hope, and Michael. He's a boy and all the rest of us are girls. That makes him the hair.'

'You mean he's the heir?'

'Well, that's what I said. Would you stand up and turn around, please?'

He shrugged his shoulders, stretched himself up to his feet, and turned around slowly. When he faced them again he smothered a chuckle and tried to look as solemn as they did.

'Hope? He's big enough, ain't he?'

'Yeah, he's big enough. He's almost as big as Daddy. Would he do?'

'Well, I dunno. She's awful choosy. Do you work, mister?'

'Yes, in a way,' he offered. 'I'm writing a book. Do you read?'

'Of course,' Faith snapped. 'I'm nine years old, f'goodness' sakes. Hope reads too, but only little words. She's only six. And Michael, he don't do nothin'—except get in trouble. He's three.'

'Poor Michael. Henpecked is he, with two big sisters?'

'Four big sisters,' Faith corrected him. 'Mattie ain't here. She goes to a big school in Boston—M.I.T., or something like that. She wants to be an engineer like Daddy.'

'She don't wanna be no engineer like Daddy,' Hope broke in with a slight lisp. 'Daddy builds roads and things. Mattie wants to build buildings, and like that. Do you make much money from writing books?'

'Well——' he drawled it out, 'not much. Just enough to live in genteel poverty.'

'It don't matter,' snapped Faith. 'Money don't matter. Not to Becky.'

'Aha,' he teased. 'Becky is the fourth sister? Where's Becky?'

'Up at the house.' Faith waved a small hand in the direction of the house above them on the hillside. 'That's why we're glad to see you. Becky's been sick, you know. She went to that crazy place where it's hot all the time and a 'squito bit her, and she's been sick and we're taking care of her. But Mommy had to go to Boston——'

'To be sworn at,' Hope interjected. 'They said that Ma had to go to the Governor's place, and he was going to swear at her. Whatcha think about that?'

'I'm not really sure,' he chuckled. 'Becky is up at the house there, and your mother had to go to Boston to be sworn at? Does Becky need help?'

'Well, maybe not right this minute,' Faith returned, 'but you can't tell with these 'squito things. She might need help any minute. That's why we thought we would check you out, you know. You look strong enough. And the three of us can't pick her up. Becky's a big girl.'

'Hey, let's not waste any time,' he said. 'If Becky needs to be picked up, we'd better go pick her up!'

'If you say so,' Faith returned. There was a mischievous smile lurking at the corners of her tiny mouth. She offered him her hand, and they all started up the trail.

They had gone no more than twenty feet when the little boy plumped himself down in the sandy soil and looked up at them with a big smile. 'Horsy,' he said. The word was very distinct, very clear.

'I thought he couldn't talk', the man said.

His sister shook the little boy's arm. 'He can talk all right, when he wants to,' she reported solemnly.

'Oh? You know what he wants?'

'Of course. He wants somebody to pick him up and carry him on their shoulders.' Faith gave a long bitter sigh, the kind of sigh one gives when being so obviously put upon. She leaned down and offered both hands to the baby, but he squirrelled backwards on the seat of his little shorts. 'Man,' he insisted.

'See?' Faith was disgusted. Her sister Hope shook her head in agreement. 'He wants *you* to pick him up. He gets a better ride when a man carries him. Say, I don't know your name.'

'No, you don't, do you,' he laughed. The little boy came eagerly to him. 'My name is Jake Meadows. Up you come, little Michael.' The child screamed in glee as he was hoisted up to Jake's shoulders, and installed as if he were riding an elephant. He pounded with his fists, kicked his heels, and yelled, 'Go! Go!'

The solemn little girl and her smaller sister looked up at them, perhaps a little enviously. 'I'm Faith Latimore and this is my sister Hope, and Becky's—well, you'll see in a minute. You must excuse my brother. He's spoiled. We can't do nothin' with him, except for Ma and Mattie. He does everything they tell him.'

'I see. Mattie is the disciplinarian?'

'I dunno what that means. Mattie is the smart one. She's in college already, and she's only just seventeen. Mattie's smart!'

'Okay.' He tried to conceal the laughter, but was not doing very well. 'Okay, I think I've got it now. Your mother is being sworn at in Boston, and Mattie is the smart one, and you three are Faith, Hope, and Michael, and Becky needs to be picked up. Is that it?'

'Weeelll!' The two girls stared at each other, exchanging messages with their eyebrows. 'Well, that's close enough for now. You are big, aren't you? Almost as big as Daddy, 'cept you're too skinny.'

They resumed their stroll up the hill. Jake kept his

strides short, to stay with the company. Michael beat on his head in a steady rhythm, trying to make him go faster. 'That's what's missing,' he chuckled. 'What about your dad?'

'Oh, he had to go to Peru,' Faith reported. 'They have a revolution, and they knocked down one of Daddy's bridges, and that made him mad, so he went down to talk to them.'

'Yes, I see,' he chuckled. 'You don't suppose the rebels might say something nasty to your dad?'

'Huh!' snorted Hope. 'You don't know my Daddy. Nobody talks back to my Daddy!'

'Well, she don't know,' the older girl reported. 'She's only six. Mama talks back to Daddy, but she makes us all go out of the room when she does it.'

'Ah,' he commented. They came around a bend in the track, and the big house was in front of them. 'The hand that rocks the cradle rules the world?'

'We don't got no cradle.'

'Now, where is this Becky who needs picking up? We'd better move a little faster.'

'Around back at the swimming pool, but I don't think hurrying will help.'

The house was an extended log cabin, with what looked to be new wings added to the centre square, all of log. Three chimneys divided the roof. Unpainted, the central section looked to be decades old, while the wings still bore the axe-marks of recent construction. He measured it all in one glance, then bent over to set the little boy on his feet.

'Now, Hope, can you keep Michael out of trouble for a few minutes? I want Faith to come and help.'

'Of course I can,' the stubby little creature returned. 'C'mon, Michael, we'll go check the freezer.'

'Ice-cream,' the little boy stated with much enthusiasm. The pair of them started off, hand in hand, for the front door.

'Now,' said Jake, turning to Faith. 'Did Becky hurt herself by falling down or something?'

There was a wary look in the child's eyes as she pondered her answer. 'No, not exactly. I told you about the 'squito, didn't I?'

'You mean "mosquito". They're big up here, but not big enough to knock somebody down.' As they talked she was leading him around the side of the house. He stopped in surprise. A classic Olympic-sized swimming pool filled the cleared area behind the house. On the near side it bordered on a sheltered patio. On the far side, outside a cement walkway, the scrub brush of the pine forest encroached. And in the middle of that walkway on the far side of the pool a lovely crumpled female body lay apparently unconscious, stretched out on a towel. He stopped, stunned. He had seen many a female body in his thirty-five years, but this one was different. 'That's Becky?' he asked in surprise.

'You bet,' Faith giggled. 'What do you think?'

What do I think? he asked himself. She was tall, and slender as a reed, with gaunt ribs showing above the minimal bikini she wore. The projecting bones seemed to emphasise the lush rounded breasts, the oval face, the luxuriously curly raven-black hair that tumbled down around her shoulders. What do I think? She looks like some abused doll!

'I think—it's strange that the rest of you are all light skin and fair hair. Your sister has an olive complexion, and the blackest hair I've ever seen! I think—oh, what the hell. Look, Faith, you go ahead into the house and find a bed or a sofa or something, and I'll carry her in. Okay?'

'Well—maybe she won't like it to be carried in. That was your idea, remember.'

'Okay, I remember. Scoot!' Faith looked up at him again, her blue eyes assessing him against some unknown goal. He patted her head and broke into a dog-trot which quickly carried him around the curved poolside. And as he moved, his computer-brain clicked on. How much time have I already wasted, coming up here to this so-called abandoned camping area? Out of the way it certainly was. It stood within the cup of the Berkshire hills, a sparkling little jewel of a lake, the tiniest shoreline, all walled in by the enormous cliffs, which guarded in every direction except the west.

A narrow gap, just wide enough for the feeder-river to escape, lay five miles to their west. An unimproved single-track dirt road hung precariously on its shoulder. It all guaranteed seclusion, and lord knew he needed seclusion or this book was just never going to get off the ground. Seclusion and quiet, that was what he needed. Not raven-haired dolls who needed to be picked up!

He had come into the camp area just before sunset of the previous day, his ancient truck bouncing all the way. It had taken him three hours to clear out the fireplace in his one-room cabin, and another two to gather firewood. In the dark, of course. It was too much to have expected moonlight. And, so, late to bed. And as soon as everything man-made became quiet, his ears had been assailed by the noises of the night. The crickets chirped all night. Two owls were evidently nesting in the eaves of the roof. Fieldmice scuttled across the floor. And then that mad baying in the distance—coyote, or just a good hound dog gone wild?

But the morning—this morning—was enough to pay for the miseries of the night. Bright sun dappled the cabin windows. A slight breeze drove off the cover of morning mist on the lake. He took a quick dip in the icy water, *sans* bathing trunks. A good breakfast. How long had it been since he had cooked over an open fire? Too long! And then out to improve his supply of firewood. All of which led to this. At this rate, he told himself wryly, I'll finish the damn book by next Christmas—if I'm lucky.

By that time he had circled the pool and was standing

at the head of the woman sprawled on the towel. Lord, look at that! his mind yelled at him. About five foot eight or nine, perhaps. I wonder what colour her eyes are? Tall, for a girl, but she needs feeding up. Her face is all bones, and her skin—there's almost a yellow tinge to it. His mind fumbled for a diagnosis. No signs of blood. She's breathing shallowly but steadily. Check for broken bones.

He squatted down beside her, and ran his hands lightly up each of her legs in turn, with practiced skill. Nothing broken, so far. He turned around, testing her rib-cage, up over her full breasts, around the slender neck. She stirred, but did not regain consciousness. With infinite care he slid one arm under her thighs, straightened his knees, and stood up with her. Not too heavy, he panted to himself. One hundred pounds—probably less?

He swung his load around and took one step towards the house, when one of those eyes opened. Dark. Deep dark eyes, to match her hair. And that was about all the time he had for reasoning.

'Just what the hell do you think you're doing!' The voice was low, well modulated, concise, and fierce!

'Why, I——' he started to explain, and then realised he had no explanation to offer. The woman in his arms began to beat on him with one tight fist. The other was clutching his back. He ducked away from the next series of blows, failed to allow for the steady kicking of her feet against his legs, and very abruptly they both fell over the edge and into the pool.

Common sense told him to kick away from her and come up for air. But the woman had evidently not read the same book. Both her arms snaked around his neck. She submerged him as she clawed at his shoulders. He let her go, easily holding his breath until her flailing feet were clear of him, and then came up to the surface himself. The woman was in the middle of the pool, doing a determined dog-paddle, but not getting very far with it.

Jake blew out to clear his nose and mouth. He was facing the house when Faith came running out at full speed, leaving the screen door to bang behind her. The girl was shouting at him. With two lazy strokes he glided over to the side of the pool and looked up at her.

Faith was almost screaming by this time. 'Get her! Get her! Becky isn't swimming!'

It took a moment for things to fall into place, a moment when he hung there on the lip of the pool and stared. And then it hit him. 'She can't swim!' He pushed off the concrete, made a diving turn, and came up near the middle of the pool. There was nothing in sight.

'Over there!' screamed Faith, pointing to the furthest corner of the pool. He took a deep breath and ducked under the surface again. Through the green haze of the water he could see a pair of feebly splashing feet.

He went after them like a shark, diving beneath her and coming up in front of her. For all the welcome he got, he might as well be a shark, he told himself grimly. He put his arms around her, with her head above water, and for some reason she kept scratching and clawing at him, pushing him under. He fumbled against her, running short of air. Two of his fingers became entangled with her bikini top. In the struggle the tiny cups fell off and floated away.

I've got to get some air, he told himself frantically. This isn't the way things are supposed to go! Driven by desperation, he struggled to the surface and snatched a breath of air. Her face was above his, and he could read the glaring rage in those deep dark eyes. Go for it, buddy, he told himself. His right arm came up out of the water in a classic short jab and hit her squarely on the chin. She collapsed against him. And now, he told himself, things can go according to the rescue book. He rolled her over on her back, cupped her shoulder with one arm, and began to shuttle them both towards the ladder at the lower end of the pool. The side-stroke had never been his favourite means of propulsion, and his arm hurt where the mortar shell had loaded him with shrapnel.

Faith was waiting for him at the poolside, and helped him push the inert girl up on to the concrete. He climbed out as quickly as he could, and made another quick check of the victim. There still seemed to be nothing wrong with her. She was breathing well, but there was a distinct bruise at the point of her chin.

Hope and the little boy joined them. It seemed like some sort of autopsy, with four of them circling the victim. 'Hit her?' the little boy asked through a moustache of chocolate ice-cream.

'She won't like that,' Hope said solemnly. 'She won't like that at all.' Her older sister shrugged her shoulders.

'Well, it's too late now,' she sighed. 'I guess you'd better carry her into the house.'

Jake could feel that warning sensation creeping up his spine. Somehow or another, he told himself, I've been had! What in the world is going on around here? He took a quick check of the three solemn children, and then back to the dark-haired girl lying at his feet. Sister? Impossible. There was not a single mark of similarity. Oh, brother!

He squatted down beside her, slipped his hands beneath her at shoulder and thigh, and stood up, taking her weight with him as a professional weight-lifter would. It took a moment to re-establish his equilibrium, and then another to remind himself where he was. He could hardly help but stare. Her head dropped back over his shoulder, stretching the muscles of her chest and stomach, and thrusting those two proud firm breasts up at him as if in challenge. Close enough to taste! Close enough to——

'And she ain't gonna like that, neither,' Faith broke in. 'You wasn't supposed to undress her. Michael, go get the other half of Becky's suit.'

'Hey, not the baby,' he started to say, but tiny

phlegmatic Michael had already kicked off his rubber clogs and dived into the pool. He swam like a dolphin— underwater mostly, popping up for a breath when it struck his fancy.

Jake looked down at the girl in his arms, and then out to where the baby boy had just completed his rescue mission. 'You can all swim?' There was more of inquisition in the question than simple interest.

'Of course.' Faith moved away from him, as if measuring him again. 'Ma taught us all before we were three years old.'

'So how come Becky can't swim?'

'Well, first of all, Becky's a Chase, you know. And she's got a mean temper. When you threw her into the swimming pool she must have thought you was attackin' us, so she was trying to drown you. Or somethin' like that!'

'That's a pretty slim story,' he accused.

'Well, Becky bein' a Chase and all, you know. She's an adopted Latimore.'

'I don't know a damn thing,' he snapped. 'And I don't think I want you to explain.' He stomped over to the end of the pool, where Hope was giving her brother a hand getting out of the water. The boy handed up the bikini top, but both Jake's hands were too occupied to take it. 'It's too wet, anyway,' he snapped, feeling as if he were looking at sour grapes. 'Lead the way. We need to get her down someplace.'

They went across the patio into the house in elephant style, Michael first, Hope next, himself, and Faith bringing up the rear. For some reason he felt embarrassed. Lord knows you've seen enough half-naked women, he hammered at himself. So why are you bugged by this one?

He fastened his eyes on the house ahead of him. On the unpeeled log finish, the mortar stuffed between the logs, the neat axe-fashioned joints as one log overlay another.

Anything to keep from looking. But at every step his eyes wavered, stole a fleeting glance at those taut firm breasts, bobbing slightly as his feet hit the ground. For God's sake! he roared at himself. Watch the stairs. Look at the chimneys. Look any place but down, damn you!

He stubbed a toe on the first step, danced up the next two still mumbling under his breath, and shouldered his way into the kitchen. The screen door slapped shut behind him with a thud.

'Up here,' Faith indicated. The procession turned to the right and up a set of plain wooden stairs, then into a room at the end of the stairs. The slanted roof threatened him. Only within the space of the single dormer window could he stand straight. The room was dimly lit. A brass double bed took up most of the space. Faith stripped back the blankets and Jake deposited the girl, still unconscious, in the middle of the bed and then pulled a sheet up over her. He felt an instant sense of relief. Stepping back, he bumped his head on the inside edge of the dormer, and collapsed into the chair by the window. His arms had felt the weight. Too many days without a workout, he told himself as he massaged his right forearm. She's a big girl. Now what?

The three little Latimores were lined up on the opposite side of the bed, watching him solemnly. 'Towels,' he snapped. 'We can't let her lie there soaking wet. And we need to find out what the original problem was. Faith, did she fall down, or something like that?'

'We'll get the towels,' the little girl announced, 'and then we'll dry Michael off.'

'Why do I keep getting the impression that there's something funny going on here?' asked Jake, but the tail end of the procession was already out the door. He shook his head and settled back into the chair. The dark beauty before him stirred but did not open her eyes. He reached into his shirt pocket for a cigarette and found a soaked pack. For the first time it came to him that he was as wet as all the others. Soaked clear down and through his old boots. Everything dripped. He pulled his shirt off over his head and threw it aside. The boots were laced with rawhide. His fingers hardly managed a grip.

There was a flurry at the door. 'Towels,' Hope announced as she tossed them at him and disappeared.

'Hey!' he called, and the girl turned around at the door. 'Gotta fix Michael,' she said, and was gone before he could get in another word. *Alice in Wonderland,* Jake told himself. But the towels were real. Somewhere in the outside distance he could hear a car motor. He brushed the curtains aside from the window but saw nothing. His hands had automatically picked up a towel and were massaging his short wet hair.

That's something I can do, he told himself. He went back to the bedside, kneeling down to protect his head, and stripped the sheet back. She was stirring slightly, moving into a foetal ball. He grabbed two of the towels and began to wipe her down gently. The bottom of her swimsuit was like a sponge, wet no matter how much he tried to dry it. Oh, brother, he told himself. In for a penny? His clumsy fingers plucked at the strings that held the tiny patch of cloth. The knots parted easily. He pulled everything free and replaced it with a towel.

Keep your hands on the towel, he told himself. Discipline, mate! But it was hard, especially when he moved up across her flat stomach and under the curve of those magnificent breasts. Lord, that was the only word that fitted—magnificent! Somehow the towel slipped, and his fingers continued.

'And she ain't gonna like that, neither,' the voice at his elbow commented. He took a quick look. Faith was there, eye to eye. He snatched both hands back, then wondered why *he* should feel so guilty. The little girl shook her head and walked around the other side of the bed. With a fresh towel, she began a vigorous massage of her sister's hair. You're being out-manoeuvred, Jake told himself. Go on the offensive, man. If this little sister can tie you up in knots, what happens when the Sleeping Beauty wakes up?

'I don't see any bumps or bruises or blood,' he said accusingly.

'Well, I never said there was any,' the child retorted.

'You—you said that——'

'All I really said,' the girl interrupted, 'was that Hope and Michael and I couldn't pick her up. I didn't say she *needed* to be picked up. *You* said that. And why ever you picked her up and threw her into the swimming pool, I don't understand. And then you hit her! Oh, my, this has just not been our day, that's what.'

'Hey, wait a minute, kid,' he snapped. 'What are you telling me?'

'Me? Tell you? I'm only a nine-year-old kid. How could I tell you nuthin'?'

'Don't give me that, Machiavelli. That body of yours might be only nine years old, but you—inside there—you're a couple of thousand years old, and don't try to tell me any different!' His legs were creaking from all the strains. He knew how lucky he was that his legs worked at all, but now he needed those pain pills, and they were back at his cabin. It was hard to think clearly.

'Well, I don't think you're very polite at all,' the child snapped at him. 'It's very plain that you just won't do!'

'Won't do what?' he growled. He took a couple of threatening steps around the bed in the general direction of this little hornet who was stabbing him to death with words. The little girl ducked away from him, just as the dark beauty on the bed began to stir. Jake stopped in mid-motion at the foot of the bed and watched. The long legs stretched, kicking the rest of the sheet aside. The arms came down and cradled her breasts, and the eyes opened in astonishment. Opened and glared at him.

'What are you doing here?' Still the low contralto voice, deepened with authority. 'Just who in the name of heaven are you?' The words came out on a rising scale. He could actually see the anger boiling up into her face. 'Faith?'

'I don't know nothin', Becky. He lives down at the cottage near the lake, and we thought—well—he came up here and picked you up and threw you in the swimming pool, and then he jumped in and hit you on your jaw.' A pause for breath. 'And then he pulled all your clothes off, and now I don't know what he's going to do. I think he wants to hit me!'

'He'd better have another think coming,' snorted Becky. She rolled over in the bed and reached into a drawer of the night stand. At which point, with the sheet gone, she discovered that she was completely on display. She fumbled something in her hand, dived back at the bed, snatched up a sheet, and wound herself up in it. 'My God,' she muttered, 'did you do that?'

'Do what?' snapped Jake. Most of his self-control was gone and he was only two steps from hitting both of them.

'Did you take my clothes off?' Again that rising note, going so high this time that it ended in a squeak of anger.

'So what can I say?' he growled at her. 'Yes, I took that puny bikini off you—if you can call that clothing. I don't suppose you want to hear why?'

'For the usual reasons, I suppose,' the dark-haired girl snarled at him. 'Rape and pillage—that sort of thing!'

'Damn it,' he growled, 'I was playing Lochinvar, not Attila the Hun! I thought you needed help. That—that nine-year-old monster led me to believe you needed help, and then when I get up here I find out there's nothing wrong with you, and—what in hell are you pointing at me?'

It was a question he needn't have asked. In the dim light of the room she had somehow managed to tie the sheet around her, and was holding a thirty-eight-calibre pistol in both hands, pointed vaguely in the direction of his stomach. He had seen enough of them in his military service to recognise, first of all, that the thing was dangerous, and, second, that the present holder hardly knew beans about firing a gun! The muzzle was wavering in a tight circle. Both her left and right hands had a finger inside the trigger guard. She was looking partly at him and partly away, as if she were planning to close her eyes before she put pressure on the trigger.

And he would probably get killed by it all, he reasoned cynically. It's always the amateur shooter and the unloaded revolver that manage to kill people. And I'm the target! Time for a little subterfuge, man. He could hear feet tramping up the stairs behind him, and a few staccato statements from Michael, who was trying to explain something to somebody. Oh, lord, he thought, there are more of these nuts. She's got reinforcements coming up. Action time!

'She's responsible!' he roared in his loudest voice, pointing towards Faith. The girl with the gun flinched, and looked quickly at her sister, who was doing her best to hide behind a pillow. It was just enough of a diversion. He bunched his aching muscles and hurled himself over the foot of the bed. Becky closed her eyes and Faith screamed. The gun skittered away from both of them, out of sight behind the bed. Jake held on desperately with both hands as Becky kicked and scratched at him. The sheet was the first victim, bunching up in a corner of the bed and falling on the floor.

'Man,' said Michael from the doorway. 'Nice man.'

'That remains to be seen, Michael.' The second voice was another lovely contralto, this one tinged with laughter. 'Man, whoever you are,' the voice continued, and there was definitely a giggle breaking through. 'I know, after many years of association with this family, that beneath all this madness there might possibly lie some logical explanation. I would suggest that you climb off—er—get off my daughter, and see what you might possibly say for yourself!'

There was a little whipcrack at the end of the statement. Jake jerked away, as if the tip of the whip had struck him. Becky was still doing her best to scratch his eyes out, so his movement was relatively awkward. Holding her hands down, avoiding the swinging kicks, he finally managed to get both feet on the floor.

'All right, Miss Becky,' the voice from the doorway said softly. The struggling girl ceased immediately, grabbed for the sheet, and bounced out of the bed on the opposite side from him.

'And now then, young man?'

He cleared his throat and turned around. Another threesome challenged him. He groaned. Was there never to be an end to all this? Hope was standing beside a tiny but very mature woman, probably in her early forties. Slim, well built, but with some white wings in the front of her crown of blonde hair. Michael was on her other side, hiding behind her skirts. There was something familiar about the woman, but he could not pin it down.

'Well?'

'You're the lady who went to Boston to be sworn at by the Governor?' He was trying to feel his way through the morass.

'All true. Care to try again?'

'And Mattie is not here because she's only seventeen, and she's enrolled in M.I.T. as an engineer.'

'Ah, you're a family confidant, I see. And what else?'

'I'm not really sure,' he sighed. 'It even sounds crazy to me. Who are you?'

'If it will make your story come out more smoothly,' the woman laughed, 'I'm Mary Kate Latimore, the mother of all these assorted children.'

'And why would the Governor want to swear at you?'

'A slight mistranslation. Who are you?'

'Me? I'm Jake Meadows. I live down——'

'Yes, I've heard that part. You live in the cottage by the lake. And?'

'Yes, well——' He stopped to rub his itching palms. Trouble, his mind reported. Is that the one about kiss a fool or have bad luck—or both? 'I started to talk to that one——' he gestured at Faith, still hiding in the corner. 'She came to my cabin and asked a million questions, and then—somehow—I got the impression that Becky here was in trouble and needed some help. So I came up the hill, and there she was stretched out on the side of the pool.'

'Asleep,' Becky stated flatly. 'Asleep!' She moved round to the front of the bed.'

'Well, I expected an injury, and you looked like an injury, and then——'

'Thanks a lot,' snarled Becky. 'And then you threw me in the swimming pool!'

'Oh, come on, now,' he complained. 'Give me a break. I didn't *throw* you in the pool. You started to beat up on me, and I slipped and we both fell into the pool!'

'So then you swam over and knocked me out?'

'I—damn it—I swam over because your sister—that little monster there—started yelling that you weren't swimming, and I thought she meant you couldn't swim. So when I caught up to you, you began climbing all over me, and I figured you were panicking and so—I—oh, what the hell!' The dark-haired beauty was almost at his side, staring at him, and his nose was itching now. 'Damn it,' he muttered, and grabbed at her with both hands. She was raging—that is, until his lips closed on hers, walling in all the sounds trying to escape through her throat. She lay there in his arms for a moment, and then gently responded. Not with flashing passion, not with madness, but with a warm calm acceptance that surprised him—startled him. He set her down gently and rubbed wondering fingers over his own lips. 'Kiss a fool,' he murmured to no one in particular.

They were all staring at him—except for Michael. That young man had walked over by the bed and spotted the gun. 'Becky!' he wailed, in a full-throated steamship roar. 'You bad Becky, you hided my gun!' And before Jake could hurtle across the room to stop him, the baby was sitting on the floor, legs apart, with the gun clutched in both hands.

'Don't anybody move,' he said softly. Surprise the child, just a second's worth, and the damn gun will go off. Why isn't his mother worried? Or either of his sisters? What the hell is going on here?

'Bad Becky,' the boy muttered, and shoved the muzzle of the gun into his mouth. He had bitten off the muzzle and the front sight before anyone said anything.

'Not too much,' his mother warned. 'All that chocolate will make you sick again, young man.' The baby looked wistfully at the rest of the gun, then struggled up and carried it over to his mother.

Out of the corner of his eye Jake could see the blush starting somewhere around Becky's knees and running up into her startlingly black hair. He turned on one heel and glared at her.

'A fake illness, an Olympic swimming record, a quick shell game, and a chocolate gun,' he grated. 'Why, I ought—I—oh hell, how did I get in this crazy mess?'

'Nice man,' said Michael from the shelter of his mother's skirt.

From behind them Faith tried one more time. 'My mother's a judge in the Superior Court,' she snapped at him.

'Now, missy!' That whipcrack again. Faith fell silent.

'What you are suggesting, Mr Meadows, is that my daughter Faith has been somewhat loose with the truth, and that you are indeed the innocent bystander?'

'Hell, I don't know what I am,' he returned. 'Go ahead, put the handcuffs on me.'

'That's only in the movies,' the judge returned. That

faint giggling smile was hanging at the corner of her mouth. 'I think we'll just adjourn court to the kitchen and have a hot cup of coffee.'

An hour later, knowing that he had been carefully 'stroked' but enjoying the sensation, Jake went out of the front door, heading for his own cabin. He stopped at the edge of the porch for a moment. Faith, Hope, and Michael. The tiny thing who claimed to be their mother. That breathtaking girl, Becky? And the missing Mattie? He chuckled, thinking sympathetically of the poor madman who was responsible for them all. Gone to Peru to lecture the guerillas! No wonder they're all mad! He stepped off the porch and almost jumped out of his skin. From behind the bushes in the front yard he heard a whistle, followed by a hiss.

'Over here!' the whisper called. He looked carefully around, but there was no one in sight. 'Over here.' The voice was a little stronger. He covered the ground in four strides.

'Oh, lord,' he muttered, 'not you again!'

'Yes, me,' Becky returned very formally. She stood up, brushing her slacks off. 'I wanted to explain.'

'Your mother has been explaining. I don't think——'

'Ma's too busy. She doesn't know beans about what's going on, and I don't want you to leave with any false impressions.' She said it all as if this were to be his final appearance; as if he were making a grand farewell. The idea brought a smile to his lips.

'You needn't laugh,' she said soberly. 'You're not exactly one of my most favourite people—you must know that. And it's hard enough for me to tell you, without you laughing!'

Jake made a wiping motion with one hand across his face, and did his best to muster up some solemnity. Her jet-black hair was dishevelled, her thin face determined, and her lush figure hidden by loose blouse and slacks. But he remembered. He licked his lips. 'So, okay, I'm not

high on your list of admirable people. What is it you want
to explain?'

'Faith,' she said mournfully. 'I've always loved my
sister, but sometimes she can be a hard cross to bear.'

'I could see that.' He was having trouble with the
corners of his mouth. 'And?'

'Well, to put it in perspective,' she sighed, 'Faith has
always been a romantic. She spends a lot of time with our
housekeeper, Alice Gimble. And Alice is a romantic too.
She keeps feeding the child with all that eighteenth-
century mumbo-jumbo, and Faith *believes* it.'

'And your mother?'

'Ma's pretty busy—you must see that. And besides——' The giggle broke through, that stupid teenage
giggle that she had spent years trying to suppress. Career
women don't giggle, for God's sake! She swallowed hard.
'To tell the truth,' she struggled on, 'Ma's a romantic
herself!'

'But you're not, of course?'

'Of course!' Very quietly said, as if it were the absolute,
but regrettable truth. 'So that's why she takes seriously
things the rest of us laugh about. Like Michael being the
heir apparent because he's the only boy.'

'And he's not?'

'Well, of course he is! The only boy, I mean. But as for
the rest of it, Pop has already arranged for all of us to
share in the Corporation, and the way Mattie is going, I
suspect she'll be its kingpin one day.'

'Not you, of course?'

'No, not possibly me. I don't know a thing about
construction.'

'You don't mean to tell me that all this foolishness is
over the idea that Faith expects Michael to inherit
everything?' Becky stretched up to her full height. Nice,
he thought. Just right. I'm tired of dealing with these
shrimps. But something more than Faith bothers this
one. Some deeper trouble. I wonder what?

'No,' she said, searching slowly for the right words. 'The problem is that I'm—well, I'm twenty-seven years old.'

'That's a nice age.'

'Well——' Her hands were busily twisting themselves into knots behind her back. 'For some things,' she sighed. 'But look at it from Faith's point of view. She thinks that marriage is the only real goal in life—for a woman. That's nonsense, but what can we say? And she also thinks that *she* can't get married until Mattie and I do. Now Mattie is only seventeen, so that's no problem, but me——'

'So Faith thinks you're the key to the log-jam. And you don't agree with her about the importance of marriage?'

'For some women,' Becky said reflectively. 'I'm sure it's nice—for my mother and father, for example. I'm a career woman, but I would probably give it all up like a shot if I met another man like Pop!'

'And in the meantime?'

'And in the meantime, my sister Faith doesn't run my life. I do that for myself!'

'I take it you don't know too many men?'

'I don't mean that.' After all, how could she explain it to him? Women doctors were still not all that thick on the ground in New England, and pushing yourself through medical school when you're not the brightest of scholars leaves little time for socialising. You got to see a large number of men, of course, but mostly they were bits of anatomy, lying stretched out under the surgeon's knife. Which didn't exactly lead to socialising, despite what the novelists claim. Certainly, in those days that seemed centuries ago, Ma had clued her in very carefully, but there's such a large gap between knowledge and experience. And how do you tell a virile man that? So she didn't.

'Besides, I don't have time for such things just now,' she said. That touch of hail and farewell again, Jake thought. What this girl needs is a good kissing.

The thought translated into action. He pulled her close against him, tilted her chin, and kissed her gently on those lovely lips. She struggled, pushing against his hard frame with her long slender-fingered hands. He smiled, applied a little more pressure to hold her in position, and returned to the assault. She continued the struggle; he reciprocated with more pressure, both of arms and lips. Her mouth opened slightly, just enough to allow him to penetrate. Nothing loath, he went on, pleased to add another scalp to his long line of conquests.

When he discovered his mistake it was about three seconds too late. Her mouth had opened, but not in passion and surrender. Rather, she was on the attack. Her gleaming white teeth slammed shut on his lower lip, and he could taste the blood.

'Dammit all to hell,' he muttered as he set her aside. 'You didn't have to bite me!'

'Yes, I did,' she snapped. 'You didn't have to try to kiss me! I only wanted to apologise for my sister. There was no need for you to attack me!' There was enough chill in her tone to freeze the lake.

'I can't say I agree,' Jake muttered through his handkerchief. 'It's pretty hard *not* to attack you. Look at that! My mouth will be swollen for a week. I could get rabies!'

'Put some cold water on it,' she advised, all practicality. 'Or try sucking on a piece of ice.'

'Yes, I accept your apology,' he muttered, 'and I hope I don't earn any more of them. Goodbye, Miss Becky—that *was* all, wasn't it?'

'I——' She was word-searching again, not wanting to send him off coldly, and yet not wanting to encourage him. 'It—isn't important,' she added quietly. 'I'm sorry if I—upset you. Goodbye.'

He looked back in the gathering twilight when he reached the turn in the path. The woman was still standing there, watching.

'And what a day this has been!' he muttered to his empty cabin as he dropped on to the rough cot. He closed his eyes and stretched out. The lovely face of Becky Latimore flashed up on the inner side of his eyelids, and haunted him all through the night.

CHAPTER TWO

ALL the Latimores shared breakfast the next morning, and then it was time for packing. 'You're positive you want to stay over, Becky? It might be lonely up here.' Mary Kate was supervising the packing, but kept a keen eye on her oldest daughter as she did so. 'There's plenty you could be doing back in Eastboro, you know. Summer is long and quiet in the country.'

'Oh, Ma,' the girl laughed, 'your idea of a long quiet summer is go-go-go. And I won't be lonely, not a bit.'

'Nevertheless—I don't really know anything about your Mr Meadows, and I hesitate to leave you here alone. Now, if you had someone from the family—well. And just because I'm leaving the jeep here it doesn't mean that you're well protected.'

'And the radio,' added Becky, doing her best to suppress the giggles. 'Look, Ma, I'm a graduate of one of the finest schools in the country. I've just spent a year's internship in a hospital tent between two armies in Chad. And when I end this vacation there'll be another grind in some hospital for my residency. Besides, I had you to tell me all about life, remember?'

'Ah, but that was before I married Mr Latimore,' Mary Kate laughed. 'I've learned a lot since then!'

'But I'd still like to stay, Ma.'

'And you still need someone around the house!'

'Well, you may be right,' Becky teased. 'And I'll agree provided I can choose for myself. Bargain?'

'There's something definitely fishy about all this— but—well, to keep us all happy, I accept. Name your candidate.'

'I think I'll choose—let me see now—Faith. How's that, Ma?'

'How's that what?' her mother responded absent-mindedly. 'Faith! That's like the blind leading the blind!'

'Why not, Ma? With Mattie away at summer school, and Hope and Michael promised for the summer with Henry's family, all we have to dispose of is Faith. She can stay here with me, and that takes care of the whole family. Right?'

'Disposed of? Why?' Mary Kate was smiling, but caution lurked behind the smile. Since Becky and Mattie had reached adulthood, Mary Kate was finding herself too often being overwhelmed by her own children.

'Think about it,' Becky insisted. 'All those beautiful *señoritas* in Peru, and the only loose male is your husband. Wouldn't you like to be there? Come on, lady!'

'This is beginning to look like a put-up job!'

'You mean you don't want to go and be with Pop?'

'I don't mean any such thing,' her mother replied quickly. ' You know darn well I'd rather be with—I mean, how in the world are you going to take care of Faith? You'll have to watch her like a hawk.'

'You've got it all wrong, Ma. She thinks she's already forty years older than I am. It'll be her watching *me*. This is all one fine idea, lady. Don't you think so?'

'Oh, I like the part about me—and your father. But it's you I'm worried about, dear. You need rest!'

'And I'll get it, love, with Faith watching over me. This could be your second honeymoon!'

'Why——' Mary Kate spluttered. Words had finally failed her.

'Don't forget,' Becky added, 'I'm the doctor around here, and I prescribe complete bedrest for you, starting at once!'

'Why, the nerve of you!' Mary Kate chuckled. 'You doctors don't know everything. Complete bedrest is what got us stuck with Michael.' But even as she argued, her

hands were busy taking the baby's clothes out of the
bureau and piling them in her case. Which was just the
cue for Michael to wobble into the bedroom with a stern
face.

'No go,' he squeaked angrily. 'Stay with Becky!'

'Speak of the devil!' laughed Becky as she picked up
the little boy and cuddled him. 'Stay with Uncle Henry,'
she whispered in the boy's ear. His head came up. His
mother had a concern for children's teeth, and rationed
sweets. But Uncle Henry was a dairy farmer who
believed in all kinds of milk products for kids—
especially icecream.

'Stay with Unca Henry,' he agreed amiably.

'See?' Mary Kate was trying to sound serious, but the
sparkle in her eye was a dead giveaway. 'That child will
be twenty years old before he finishes a sentence!'

'C'mon, Ma,' Becky chided. 'We don't have to look
very far to find out who pampers him the most.'

'Well, of course you don't,' her mother sighed. 'It's
his father, that's who.' She raised her voice to be heard
around the house. 'Get a wiggle on, girls. That helicopter
is due in twenty minutes, and you know how your father
feels about people who keep his helicopters waiting!'

It took a dozen more chidings before they were ready
to go. Everyone but Michael carried a case as they started
down the path, Indian file. Jake Meadows was out in
front of his cottage as they went by. He stopped his busy
work to wave.

'Leaving?' It was a rhetorical question, and Becky
could feel the tone beneath the words. Why, damn the
man, she thought. I dreamed about him all night, and
he's *happy* that we're leaving. Happy! He wants the
whole area to himself.

Becky and Michael were in the middle of the column,
Faith in the rear. 'Goodbye, man,' the boy called.

'Goodbye, Michael. Goodbye, Becky,' he returned.
There was more than a little sarcasm in that second

salute. Becky did her best to glare him down, but he was glare-proof. His broad sun-tanned face split wide apart in a grin that showed strong white teeth. She nodded coolly to him, and tugged at Michael's hand. Wait until we come back, she threatened him silently. Wait until all the *nice* people go off, and he discovers who they've left behind. Whom?

'Nice man,' said Michael, and then, because Becky made no answer, he repeated it over and over like some liturgical chant. She shook his hand with the tiniest bit of impatience.

'Don't say that,' she commanded fiercely. It was the first real opposition that Michael could remember, and he set about remedying the situation. He dug both feet into the sandy path, and the tears started to flow.

'Nice man,' he repeated, and dropped on his bottom, refusing to go another step. Overhead Becky could hear the rattle of the approaching helicopter as it swooped in low over the northern peaks and aimed for the only clear landing area, the beach itself. She knew when she was beaten. She put down the suitcase she was carrying, swept her little brother up in her arms, and hugged him.

'Yes, nice man.' She tried to make her surrender softly, but a quick glance back up the trail showed that he had heard every word, and was thoroughly enjoying himself.

'Damn!' Michael cried a little harder. 'It's all right, Michael. He's a nice man—a nice, nice man.' The tears were shut off immediately. But when she tried to set him down on his own feet he would have none of it. His tiny arms came around her neck and clung like a leech.

'Loves Becky,' he mumbled into the base of her neck.

'And Becky loves Michael,' she returned. The helicopter had already landed, and she could see a crewman drop out of the doorway to help with the baggage. She shifted the boy higher in her arms, resting his head on her shoulder, patting his back for comfort. Which took two hands.

'Let me help you.' She could hear the glee in his voice. Damn the man, she told herself. He's so eager to see me gone that he's willing to carry all the luggage. There was no way she could refuse the help. Her mother was gesturing from the open door of the helicopter, and Hope was being helped inside.

'Thank you,' she said, not at all gracefully. And he knew it. He picked up the suitcase as if it were a feather and made a broad, sweeping motion down the path.

'After you, lady.' If there had been even a semblance of a grin on his face as he said that, Becky would have dropped the baby and hit him. Instead, after swallowing her bile, she looked at him haughtily, and gave another cold 'Thank you'. That was when he laughed.

It was too late for her to do anything spectacular, because he was urging her on down the trail from behind, leaving her nothing to do but to clutch the child close and hurry along.

The pilot had left his engine on and the blades revolved slowly in the idle position. The noise was deafening. Meadows passed the suitcase up to the waiting crewman, then turned to offer the same service to Becky. She passed the child to him. He turned and handed the child up to Mary Kate, then offered Becky a hand again.

She was caught in a spasm of giggles. She backed away from the helicopter, taking Faith with her. The crewman slammed the big sliding door shut. 'Hey, you forgot——' Jake Meadows shouted, but the rest of his words were lost in the roar of the chopper's engine. He sprinted a yard or two in Becky's direction and then turned to look as the big machine grumbled into the air. There was an astonished look on his face. He continued to watch until the helicopter cleared the eastern cliffs, and even its noise was gone.

It was hard not to giggle. Becky carefully folded her hands behind her as she watched. For a moment, it looked as if he were trying to recapture the helicopter. Then his back stiffened, and he turned around very slowly.

'I suppose this means that you two are going on a later flight?'

'I guess you might say that,' Becky returned sweetly. Her hand toyed with the tight curls of of her hair. Faith had already stalked up the hill, out of sight.

'I don't suppose you'd care to tell me exactly when?'

'I don't know that I know, exactly,' she responded. 'It depends on a lot of things. Like when Pop comes back from South America. And when Mattie finishes summer school. Or maybe when I get tired of rusticating up here in the woods. There are such a lot of things involved. Why do you ask?'

'Don't give me that sweet talk,' he snapped. 'I know a lot about you, lady.'

'And you sound as if you don't like what you know!'

'Hey, I don't mean it that way.' He flashed her a smile, and relaxed. 'I just find you all so confusing!'

Now that's what you call a swift change, Becky told herself. In me, not him. All of a sudden it's nice to walk in the sunshine with him! 'I can see how that could happen,' she told him. 'Let me see now. In the beginning there was Pop, and he had a daughter—that's Mattie. And on the other side there was Ma, and she had a stepdaughter—that's me. She also had a stepson, too—but Henry is ten years older than Ma, so we don't usually count him. With me so far?'

'I suppose so,' he chuckled. 'And then what?'

'And then Ma and Pop got married, and they had three children of their own. That's——'

'I know,' he interrupted. 'That's Faith, Hope, and Michael! I'll bet Michael was a surprise!'

'Well, he was,' she said solemnly, 'but we were all happy about it. There had to be somebody to carry on the name. And Ma had a hard time. She had to stay in bed for four months before Michael was born.'

'Ah! So now all we have to do is to get all the girls married off!'

Becky turned a surprised face up to him. 'I told you before—that's a bunch of nonsense, and it's none of your business!'

'And there are four of you?'

'Don't make it sound as if we're all at desperation's door,' she snapped at him. 'I have my career, and Mattie is surely going to be an engineer. You men are not indispensable!' .

'Well, don't count on that,' laughed Jake . 'We *do* have our uses now and then.'

Becky was still blushing as she rushed up the trail past his house. She almost tripped over a root, and was saved from a nasty fall by his arm. She shook him off, and took a couple of steps up the hill.

'Don't I even rate a goodbye?' he asked. She stared back at him over her shoulder, wondering what he was up to now. He looked serious, but that was no sure sign. Slowly she walked back down to his level and offered her hand. 'I don't shake hands with girls,' he said solemnly. 'Girls always get kissed goodbye.'

Becky felt frozen, unable to move forwards or backwards. His eyes were holding her, and then his arms. His warm lips touched lightly on her forehead, and then on her partly opened mouth. There was a sensation like nothing she had ever experienced before, but her determination shook it off. She beat against his chest until he released her, and then one of her hands swung at him, and landed. He blinked his eyes. She wiped her mouth with her hands. 'I told you!' she snarled at him.

'Yes, you did,' he said. 'Goodbye, Becky.'

She turned and ran up the hill as if the hounds of hell were chasing her.

It was nine o'clock before Becky was able to get Faith

settled and into bed. It took fifteen minutes of reading to lull the child into sleep. Becky looked down at her, the sprawling bud of beauty, her golden hair splashed across the pillow, and instantly recognised her own adult problem.

'That's what I want for myself,' she murmured. 'What Ma has. Love, a home, babies.' She hugged the feeling to her and went softly downstairs. The front door was open, although the screen door was closed against the multitude of bugs. The air was soft, scent-laden. She felt the urge to walk.

There was no real problem about the child; Faith, once asleep, would sleep through an earthquake, and the house was electronically wired to a child's needs. Becky stopped by the front door and turned on the 'baby alarm', an open microphone and transmitter that broadcast every twist and cough from Faith's room. One more switch transferred the sound to the outdoor amplifier, which hurled the tiniest sigh over a couple of acres of woodland.

She doused herself mightily with bug spray. Romance was great, but her disastrous encounter with the *Anopheles* mosquito during her African tour of duty had left her with great respect for the smallest of beings.

Quietly she eased out on to the porch and closed the screen door carefully behind her. She gathered up the skirts of her simple cotton dress and sat down on the porch step. Overhead she could see the evening star marshal all its companies. And on the saddle of the eastern mountain was the first gleam of a full moon.

A haunting nightingale song drifted in from the lake, and a splash or two out in deep water indicated that 'acid rain' had not yet killed this particular body of water. But soon, she told herself. Too, too soon. Discouraged at the idea she got up and started down towards the beach, following a different path from the one that led past his cabin. This one ended up at the sandiest part of the little beach. Wavelets surged in and out, splashing on the sand, beating up the pilings of the little wooden dock. Three boats were tied up there. It was too dark to see clearly. 'Two of ours,' she muttered, 'and one of his?'

There was a shadowed something at the end of the pier. Curiosity pulled her. She stopped for just a second to listen. The amplifiers back at the house were working well; she could hear deep breathing, and that little rasping snore that was typical of Faith, asleep. She turned her attention to that shadow at the end of the pier. Moving on light feet, she stalked it.

For a moment the moon rose high enough to light the cupped valley, and then a cloud blotted it out. She kept up her stalking pace, looking up to where the edges of the cloud were now moon-bright. Her unwatched right foot thudded against an uneven log. She pitched slightly forward, her knees bent, her hands out in front of her to break her fall. Somehow or other her hands glanced off flesh. She had time for just one scream before she, and the something in front of her, tumbled off the end of the pier and landed in four feet of water. With her feet firmly anchored on the bottom, Becky screamed again. There *were* bears in these mountains—not many, not very big, but some. Except that this bear in front of her talked.

'Now what in hell's half acre did you do that for!'

There was no doubt about it, he was angry. And evidently tangled up in his fishing lines, she concluded, as she listened to his mumbled curses, punctuated by a yelp of real pain. And what do you do now? she asked herself, trembling. The moon slid out from behind the cloud and splattered them both with silver. He was holding his hand up, cursing it—and her—and everything else within twenty miles. A fish-hook stood firmly imbedded in the middle of his hand.

He seemed to realise the non-profitability of struggling. His shoulders shrugged, and he seemed to withdraw into himself. 'You again, Becky Latimore?'

Well, he already knows who you are, she told herself
fiercely. It's just a rhetorical question. Should I say no?
He doesn't seem to be in a very pleasant mood. The
thought sent a shiver down her spine. So what do I say?
'You seem to have a fish-hook stuck in your hand.'

'Do I really?' She could have measured the sarcasm
with a twenty-gallon pail. 'Now how in the world could
that have happened?' More sarcasm. And then a bellow
that echoed off the cliffs and across the lake. 'My God,
woman, every time you come near me, you're trouble!
Did you hear that? Trouble. Now please get out of my
ever-loving way and go haunt some other beach!'

'You needn't be so sarcastic about it,' she muttered at
him. 'There isn't any other beach.' There was water in
her eyes—from the fall into the lake, she told herself. I
wouldn't be caught dead crying over this—this man!

'I'll be as sarcastic as I want!' he roared back at her.
'Just because we share the same planet is no reason for
me to have to wear a red warning light on my back. And
now I'll have to go all the way into the village to find a
doctor—this damn fish-hook has gone right through my
palm.'

'It does look a problem,' she sighed. 'I don't suppose
you would want me to help?'

'You've got it in one, lady. I don't want any socialite
medical aide chopping around my fingers. I need them
all for my business.' By this time Jake had extricated
himself from the mass of fishing line. He rolled it all up in
a ball, picked up his pole in the other hand, and began a
dogged wade towards the beach. Becky started to follow
him.

'Do me a favour!' he snarled. 'Stay in the water until I
get at least a hundred yards head start. More of your kind
of luck I don't need!'

She could feel the tears running down her cheeks. Look
at me! she shouted at herself. You *are* crying over him.
Fool! She mustered control of her voice.

'All right. But you won't forget that I *did* offer help?'

'Yeah, I'll remember,' he snorted. 'Probably until my dying day I'll remember. My great-grandchildren will be telling the story to *their* kids, believe me!'

He stalked up the beach mumbling to himself. She waited until he had rounded the corner of the path, and then she made her way ashore. I ought to go after him, she chided herself. Just because he doesn't want help it doesn't mean that he won't need it! But how can you help a man who hates the very sight of you? His great-grandchildren, huh! What woman would marry *him*? She felt a pain in the pit of her stomach, and used both hands to wipe away her tears. Whatever happened to that quiet restful summer I was going to spend in the Berkshires? She cocked an ear to the night noises. There was still that low-level mixture of sound, as the forest grew and played and hunted. And above it all, the deep breath and tiny snore as Faith slept on.

'Thank God for that,' she sighed. 'And I'll just see that Michael doesn't grow up to be *his* sort of man.' She would have preferred to stay on the beach, wet as she was, but niggling the back of her mind was the idea that he might *need* help. She started slowly up the path. He was behind his cabin with a lantern as she came up the hill. She stopped on the path and watched. He had cut the line loose from the hook, and, working with one hand, was doing his best to start one of the oldest trucks she had seen. And not having much luck.

'Can I help with the truck?' she offered. That shouldn't make him angry, should it? It did.

'Why don't you just damn go home?' he snarled. 'When I'm ready to start the truck, I'll start it!'

'But I think——'

He moved out of the lantern light in her direction. My God, he's going to beat me up, she told herself. It was a time for running, and she could not get her feet to move. He had left the lantern behind him as he came closer.

And for one of the few times in her life, Becky found herself looking up at a man. The idea startled her. She knew he was big, but there's a difference between close-big and faraway-big. She backed away a couple of steps, and could not help noticing his hand.

'It's still bleeding,' she said hesitantly. 'You've got to get that hook out quickly!'

'Yeah, sure,' he snapped. 'I will in a minute. Just as soon as I get you out of my sight, Miss Busybody. I said *"go"* twice. Isn't that enough for you?'

'Yes—I—but if you need help, please come to the house.' Those last few words she threw over her shoulder as her feet finally accepted her marching orders.

'Yeah,' he snorted. 'As soon as Hell freezes over!'

'It could happen,' she yelled back at him. 'Septicaemia.'

'Yeah!' he roared. He obviously meant to add something else, but Faith woke up. Her little whimper, amplified a thousand times, boomed down over brush and forest, and startled every living thing in the area. Two quail burst from cover at Becky's feet, scaring her almost as much as *he* had. And then, still amplified, Faith began to cry.

'Becky? Becky!' The slender pine forest seemed to sway to the power of the complaint. Becky sped up the path, stopping at the front door only long enough to turn off the amplifiers. The sudden cessation of mechanical sound left a total silence outside, and then the forest gradually returned to its regular life cycle. Becky raced for the stairs and into the bedroom.

'I'm here, love,' she assured the girl, nuzzling her close. The little girl was sprawled at the foot of her bed in a confusion of blankets.

'Becky,' she wailed, 'I had a terrible nightmare.'

'So did I, love, but it's all right now.'

'You're all wet, Becky.'

She fumbled for the right words. 'I went down to the

beach to see Mr Meadows, and we both fell in the lake.'

'That's funny, Becky!'

'It's not all *that* funny,' Becky told her sternly. 'Now let's try to get back to sleep, and maybe neither of us will have any more nightmares tonight.' Her sister smiled at her and ducked under the covers. Becky watched for a time, until the little body was still, and then went downstairs. Before her foot was off the bottom stair there was a thunderous knock at the front door.

'Now who?' she muttered as she changed direction. 'Bigfoot, or Bigmouth?' Her hand reached out for the knob, then she had second thoughts. 'Who is it?' she called through the closed door.

'Very funny,' the gruff voice outside retorted. 'How the hell many of us are there at this lake?'

'Well, I had to be sure,' she returned solemnly as she opened the door and stood aside. Jake Meadows strode into the light, holding one hand gingerly in the other.

'I need some help,' he growled.

'I didn't realise it was that cold,' Becky returned stiffly. 'As I remember, you didn't plan to ask my help until Hell froze over.'

'So maybe I said a few words in haste,' he half-apologised. 'I can't get my truck started. May I use your jeep?'

'Of course you may,' she returned calmly. 'But I don't think you could drive any distance with only one hand.'

'I don't see anything else to do,' he growled. A band of sweat broke out on his forehead. She walked over and picked up his wounded hand. A slow coursing of blood surrounded the shaft of the fish-hook. The point was buried deep in his flesh. She shook her head. 'I'll tell you what, Mr Meadows, why don't you let me call the nearest doctor, and see what happens?'

'I'm afraid to find out,' he returned cautiously.

'Sit down at the table,' she directed. Her manner had changed, he noticed. She was no longer an awkward girl, but rather had assumed an aura of authority. Almost without thinking about it, he let her push him into a chair. 'Wait there,' she ordered, and left the room. Becky hurried, trying to be quiet enough not to waken Faith. There was no sense adding trouble on trouble. Jake was still sitting at the table when she came back downstairs.

'You wanted the nearest doctor,' Becky told him. She had her black medical bag in one hand, and her diplomas in the other. She spread the papers out in front of him. He managed to focus an eye.

'Johns Hopkins?' The idea seemed to rock his mind. 'You're the doctor?'

'You'd better believe it,' she sighed. 'And now——'

She was about to ask him about allergies, since she had a limited choice of local anaesthetics in her bag. But the question was redundant. Before her eyes, moving slowly as one would believe the Tower of Pisa might fall, Jake leaned further and further, and eventually collapsed with his head and shoulders on the table, and his injured hand sprawled out, palm up, directly in front of her.

'That certainly proves something,' she muttered as she opened her case and laid out the necessary tools, 'but I haven't the slightest idea what it is. He's too big to collapse from the result of a simple fish-hook. Oh well, when in doubt . . .' and she reached for the hypodermic needle.

CHAPTER THREE

'IVE never seen a worse patient,' Becky told Jake as she checked his hand four days later. 'A little thing like a fish-hook, and you act as if your world had come to an end! One fish-hook and six stitches.'

'That's all right for you to say,' he grumbled, 'but the fish-hook didn't stick into *your* hand, as I recall.'

'At least you could say something nice about the treatment,' she shot back at him. 'Not even a thank-you!'

'I was waiting to see the size of the bill,' he returned. 'You do sew a nice seam. Did you ever take up knitting?'

'They don't teach that in medical school,' she said, 'but yes, I can sew and knit and crochet. And there won't be any bill. I'll just mark this off to experimental surgery.'

'Ah, no bill.' He cocked his head to one side, watching her every expression. It seemed to make him look—well, different, she told herself. In the last four days she'd been puzzled by his strange behaviour. For a man who had seemingly come to Lake Mohawk to be alone, he had been paying very regular visits.

It disturbed Becky. She wanted nothing more than to put that man, and all the chaos he had brought into her life, out of her mind—but with his turning up like this every day, she couldn't do it. For the life of her she couldn't understand why he kept coming—especially since Faith had apparently taken a great dislike to him after his poor handling of the swimming pool incident. The temperature was distinctly chilly whenever the two of them met.

She wished she could telegraph her disapproval as effectively as her sister did. The trouble was that Jake Meadows made her forget all the skills she knew for dealing with men. She couldn't treat him with the right cool sophistication, and she couldn't get him out of her mind, damn it!

'So how come you're so handy about the house?' he continued. 'You bake your own bread, make your own soups—everything first class. I don't know any other doctors with that sort of skill.'

'You don't know any other doctor who grew up under my mother's thumb, either,' Becky chuckled as she rebandaged the hand.

'You mean that nice little lady I met a few days ago? Come on now, Rebecca. Butter wouldn't melt in her mouth.'

'Believe what you want,' she laughed, 'but don't take my mother for granted. She's a sharp one, that lady. And she taught me everything a girl needs to know.' He smiled back at her, a wide smile that displayed a fine array of teeth, and two gleaming eyes.

'So, then,' he said, 'I do thank you. It's a fine job you've done for me, and I do appreciate it. Maybe we could start again from the beginning, you and I?'

It seemed like a fair offer. She looked him over from top to bottom and admitted to herself that he looked worthy of—friendship? 'Okay,' she said softly, her voice dropping to a husky contralto. She stuck out a hand and watched it being swallowed up. Her hands were not small; they matched her size, and had a surgeon's flexibility. His was a huge thing, that enveloped hers. 'Rebecca Latimore,' she told him. 'People call me Becky.'

'Meadows,' he returned. 'Jake Meadows.'

'Hey,' she warned, 'those hands are my treasure! Gently!'

His face turned red as he reluctantly let her go.

'I'm hoping to be a surgeon one of these days,' she added lightly. 'Although with all that extra study—well, I just don't know.'

He looked at her so solemnly that she could not repress a chuckle, and collapsed into one of the kitchen chairs. The outside door slammed.

'Becky! Look what I found!' Faith came bouncing in through the door, a struggling frog quivering in her hand.

'Oh dear!' Becky sighed. 'Be careful, love, or you'll scare the poor thing to death!'

'I won't,' the girl returned. 'I like animals. Is a frog an animal? Oh, hello, Mr Meadows. Are you back here again?'

'Watch what you're doing,' Jake cautioned. 'Your sister is right—that little thing could be squashed to death.' He held out his hand and Faith passed him her treasure without demur, but stepped back quickly as soon as he had the frog under control. There was a look of defiance on the child's face.

'There's nothing wrong with this frog,' Jake reported. 'Why don't you take it back to where you found it? Its family might be looking for it.'

'Frogs don't have families,' the child snapped. He looked as if he were about to say something additional, then stopped.

'I'll go with you,' Becky offered, but Faith hesitated.

'You won't have time,' Jake interrupted. 'Not if we're going fishing this morning.'

'We're going fishing this morning?' Becky glared at him. She had not the slightest memory about going fishing with him. Being friends—well, that was stretching the cloth to about its limit. But going fishing? The idea caught her so far off base that she was amazed to hear herself say, 'And why not? That might be wonderful. We haven't had any fish on the menu since we've been here. Faith, why don't you go and return the frog, and we'll all go fishing.'

'I don't wanna go,' the girl returned. 'Fishing's stupid. You can go. I want to stay here and listen to my records, and if you go fishing I can play them as loud as I want, the way they're supposed to be!'

'You're sure you don't want to go?'

'No, I don't, Becky.' Not with him, the glare she gave him said!

'Honest Injun?'

'Cross my heart and hope to die!'

They made a curious pair as they struggled down to the dock. Becky led the way, her fishing pole over her shoulder, and a lunch basket in one hand. Behind her, under the weight of oars and poles and bait cans, all balanced in one hand, came Jake.

And as they walked, Becky kept running something over in her mind. Just what am I doing, she asked for the umpteenth time. I still haven't the slightest idea who he is, what he does, or why he does it here. All I really know is—admit it—I like what I see.

It was hard to square the attraction she felt with her first conviction that she was dealing with a criminal lunatic. He'd slugged her, hadn't he? And—and *looked* at her while she lay unconscious? She might have done exactly the same to any number of male patients, but that was different—very different. And now here she was, going fishing with him just because she couldn't remember the word 'No'.

The boats were all moored at the far end of the dock, bobbing slightly in the small breeze that perfumed the valley. Becky set her load down and stepped gingerly into the flat-bottomed boat. It shifted under her weight. Out of the corner of her eye she could see Jake sauntering down the path, whistling. Not a care in the world, she thought. If there's anything that Miss Becky Latimore must accomplish today, it's to find out what Jake Meadows is. And that's an order! She clicked her heels and bowed.

The heel-clicking did it. Cold clammy water swished in the bilges, splashed over her tennis shoes, and wet her slacks. With a muttered curse she bent down and recovered the old bailing can from under the stern thwart. Jake slowed down a pace, so that by the time he arrived at the boat her work was nearly done.

It wasn't hard work, she told herself, but it really—it really was man's work! The thought brought on laughter, and she collapsed back on the stern seat and hugged herself. The boat swayed as he came aboard. Becky Latimore, she lectured herself, what would Pop say? She knew. 'There's no such thing as separate work for men and women,' he always said, 'there's just sharing.' And what was the rest of that little lecture he gave herself and Mattie at least twice a year? Oh, yes, 'And when you find someone with whom you're willing to share everything, that's love, my darlings.'

It was a nice thought. She didn't really mind sharing some things with Mr—with Jake. She took a deep breath to settle her control, and pushed her long black hair away from her face. The wind was idling gently down the lake from the west, sniffing at everything in sight as it ruffled the mirror-clear water. It tangled in her hair again, gently. She pulled a ribbon out of her pocket and tied the hair back in a ponytail. A pair of bobolinks were singing behind her, on the hill. And nothing else was happening. She looked down the length of the boat at him.

Jake was standing just forward of the middle seat. He held both oars in one hand, and he was laughing.

'You can hardly row the boat from back there,' he said pompously. Becky looked up quickly and just caught the edge of a smile.

'Row?'

'Yes. You know—propel the boat? You can't expect me to row, do you? My doctor has this thing about abusing my hand, and I'm sure she wouldn't be happy to see me rowing the boat.'

'I knew there was some catch to this trip,' she snapped. 'I'm supposed to be resting. That's what this whole vacation in the woods is all about!'

'We could share a seat and each take an oar?' Again that fleeting smile, gone before she could appraise it, leaving a smirk behind as Jake fumbled to arrange his facial expressions.

Surely, she told herself, you're not going to fall for that old gag? Share a seat, indeed! There's hardly room enough there for the two of us to squeeze in, never mind row. And he knows it. Look at that face! What a thoroughly despicable man he is. A—a wolf in sheep's clothing—that's the right phrase for him.

'Well?'

'I'll row by myself,' she sighed. He stood up and tried to balance himself *and* the boat as she slid by him. The little flat-bottomed craft rocked and swayed.

'Hey!' Becky protested. The boat shifted again as Jake worked his way aft, and that moment her left foot slipped and she fell back against the strength of him. Both his arms came around her from behind.

She felt the security of the rescue, but both his hands were dangerously close to her breasts. Dangerous for me, she told herself. It doesn't seem to bother *him* at all. 'Put me down,' she muttered.

'All right,' he returned. He leaned slightly to let her weight slip down, and as he did so his hands rode gently up over the peaks of her breasts, seemed to hesitate there for a second, then settled in her armpits. With care he lowered her to the middle seat and released her.

'There you are.'

It was perhaps just a routine comment, but Becky was having trouble with her breathing. 'Oh, lord!'

'What have I done now?'

'Nothing—I—nothing,' she stammered. 'I——' She took two deep breaths to settle herself, fumbling with the oars as she did so.

'You *do* know how to row?' There was that little touch

of sarcasm. Her spinning mind seized on it. Anger could be her armour!

'Yes,' she snapped at him. The corner of his mouth quivered. 'If you wouldn't mind sitting down?' She glared at him, trying to concentrate enough venom in a glance to poison him. It failed its mark. Jake dropped on to the broad seat, crossed one leg over the other, and made a gentle motion with his good hand, a sort of 'let's get with it, galley slave' motion. She shrugged her shoulders. It would be futile to argue. A minute or two was required for fitting the oars into the metal oarlocks. And still she waited.

'Do we have to have a signal?' he asked. More sarcasm. She noted it all down in the back of her mind. One day, retribution would come. Despicable man! She took a deep breath and leaned on her oars.

'It's a family rule,' she told him sweetly. 'Nobody takes a boat out without wearing a life-preserver.'

'Great day,' he muttered, 'this isn't an ocean voyage!'

'Under your seat,' she returned serenely. It was hard to catch his exact words as he bent over, reached between his knees, and pulled. And maybe I wouldn't want to know all those words, she told herself primly. It was hard not to laugh. How could you work in medicine as long as she had without hearing all the four-letter words that the language possessed?

Jake struggled for another two or three minutes, and finally three usable orange life-vests appeared. Becky picked out a medium-sized unit and struggled into it. There was no easy way to do the job. The strings that held it together in front of her were wet from the bilge water, and untying knots that the previous user had left in them was more than troublesome. But success comes to those who persevere—or something like that—she told herself angrily. Settling her jacket securely around her waist, she reached back up on to the dock and rescued the lunch basket and her fishing pole.

'Worse than shoeing a mule,' she muttered as she resumed her bench seat. Jake had already completed his requirements and was leaning back in his seat again, laughing. Good ears, she noted. Be careful what you say when he's around. She shrugged her shoulders again and flexed the outboard oar.

'Permission to shove off?' he asked.

'Please.' He untied the lines and gave one gentle push. At least it seemed to be gentle, but the loaded boat swept out into its own element with power and grace. Becky dropped both oars in the water, flexed her fingers, and looked at him. 'Just where are we going?'

'Wherever the fish are,' he returned.

'Sure, but there's no sign on the lake. Where's that?'

'You mean to tell me you haven't fished this lake before?'

She sighed in exasperation. 'I don't mean to tell you anything, Mr Meadows. Our family has been coming up to this lake for ten years or more. The arrangement is simple. You catch the fish, you clean them and I'll see that they get cooked. That's what my mother does. And she *never* rows the boat!'

'And your mother is perfect, of course?'

'You'd better believe it, mister. You'd better believe!'

He didn't seem to be overly impressed. He stretched his legs out in front of him and grinned at her. Becky recognised defeat: it didn't have to come to her labelled and served on a platter.

'Well, Mr Know-It-All,' she snarled, 'I'm ready. Where do we go?'

'Up north of here.' He gestured. 'There's a little island called Three Pines. The best fishing is just off the southern end.'

'But that's——'

'Only half a mile,' he said mildly. 'Shall we go?'

It took an hour to get to the island, and another half-hour before he was satisfied with the location. He did condescend to throw out the little anchor, and the boat swung round into the wind.

'You *are* going to fish?' he asked after a few minutes, when Becky had sat quietly in her seat and he had baited his own line.

'You brought worms,' she sighed.

'Of course. That's what fish like to eat. Don't tell me I've got a doctor who's squeamish about worms?'

'Not exactly,' she defended herself. 'I'm not squeamish about worms, but—I just hate to put them on the hook. And besides——' But she wasn't going to tell him the rest of it. A blister had formed in the palm of each hand. She surveyed the rest of her worn anatomy, all the while keeping an eye on him as he baited her hook. And then the lines went overboard. She started to say something to him, but he shushed her. 'Don't disturb the fish.' A typical male response, she thought as she fumbled in her little shoulder purse. But there wasn't a great deal to offer. Next time I'll stock the bag differently. *Next* time? No, no. Not ever. This one proved the adage. Three terrible failures were enough for any right-minded girl. I really don't know when I've met a more objectionable man in all my life! A writer—huh! I'll bet he writes pornography. Or those best-seller books that are wall-to-wall sex. But even that takes some brains. Maybe I'm overrating him. Maybe he writes advertisements, or something like that!

'You having trouble, Becky?'

'Me? Not at all. Why should I have trouble? Just because I've got blisters like crazy, and I'm hot and tired and thirsty, why should I have any trouble!'

'Blisters? Well, that happens. Is that why you've been talking to yourself for the last fifteen minutes?'

'I wasn't talking to myself,' she insisted. Anger hadn't seemed to help. Maybe standing on her dignity might. She pulled her shoulders back and did her best to show uninterest. Unfortunately, this pose thrust her little nose proudly up in the air, and strained the light cotton of her blouse against her bra-less breasts. Jake was laughing again. Damn the man!

Becky managed the *grande dame* approach for about two minutes, but the giggles were eating a line at both ends of her mouth, until finally they broke out of control completely.

'Hey, you really have to be quiet. You'll scare the fish away with all that noise!'

'I'm sure I will,' she snapped. Her eyes were glued to the little red bobbin tied on the end of her line. It was no longer floating level and calm in the water. Something was agitating it, something that finally pulled the little plastic ball completely underwater, and bent her pole in a trembling U-shape. She slid the butt end of the pole between her legs, using her two damaged palms gently.

'Atta girl,' Jake said softly. 'Play him now. Don't let him get back into those reeds—that's the way! Now, a little at a time, take up the line with your reel.'

'I can't hold it,' she sighed. 'My hands hurt too much.'

Instantly he was up on the thwart with her, pulling her back against him, his arms coming around her and adding more leverage to the struggle. She couldn't help it. Her breath whistled inwards in surprise, and her heart doubled its beat, almost as if she were climbing Mount Annapurna rather than sitting in a rowboat on a quiet lake. His face entranced her. She watched out of the corner of her eye. It had lost all its craggy lines, its adult worry-marks, and sparkled like that of a little boy. He was really concentrating, the tip of his tongue protruding from his mouth. The valiant fish strayed too close to the boat. The net swept him up, and in one fluid movement the fish thudded against the floorboards and flapped around.

'Oh, my God!' moaned Becky. She pulled her feet up on to the seat and out of the way. Life and death, she had seen it all, but live snakes and flapping fish were too much for her.

'My God, indeed,' Jake chuckled. He dropped the handle of the net, seized the fish in his bare hand, and removed the hook. 'A fine catch—trout, no less. That makes good eating. Three, maybe four pounds.' He tossed the fish to the bottom of the boat and reached for her hook and the bait can.

'I—I don't think I want to fish anymore,' said Becky. 'I'm—tired, and my hands hurt, and I——'

'It's okay,' he interrupted. 'Let's go ashore and see if we can't find something to ease the pain.' As he talked, he squeezed by her to the bow, heaved up the anchor, and hooked it by its flukes to the side of the boat. Her eyes followed his every move. He walked with slightly spread feet, as if he were accustomed to pitching decks. There was no wasted motion. Michael likes him, she thought. Maybe he writes very nice books? Maybe. Just one more of those questions never covered in my anatomy books. She shook her head and reached gingerly for the oars.

'No.' His big hand stopped her. 'You can't row any further with blisters like that.'

'Then how in the world do you think we're going to move?' she snapped.

'There now,' he chuckled. 'Be nice, Becky. Everyone says you're the nicest girl to come down the pike in this century. Why not try a little nice with me?'

He unshipped one of the oars and laid it out in the bottom of the boat. With the other in hand he moved to the stern, thrust the oar through a small gash in the stern bulwark, and stood up, wiggling the oar experimentally. 'It's called sculling,' he told her cheerfully. 'Would you believe it, many years ago I was the sculling champion of my school.'

'Oh, I believe it,' she returned. 'That was before they invented the canoe, wasn't it?'

He gave her a deeply hurt look. 'See,' he said. 'That's

why I get the impression that you don't like me. Whatever happened to the truce we declared in the kitchen?'

'Things are different out here in the light of day,' she snapped. 'And I didn't know then that you were going to force me to do all that rowing. I think you deliberately set out to deceive me—from the very start!'

'Why, Becky,' he laughed, leaning into the oar. 'If my memory serves, wasn't it you who invited me?' She blushed. The truth of the matter was that she just couldn't remember who did what to whom. The morning had been filled with more upsets per square mile than she knew could happen. And he knew it. Look at that gleam in his eye!

'If I did, I take it all back,' she said. 'I've been had, there's no doubt about that. And nothing makes me feel worse than to be done in by a sneaky conniving trick!'

'And that puts me in my place,' he mourned, but there was still laughter tugging at the corners of his mouth.

He's no writer, she told herself fiercely. He's an actor! The perfect Simon Legree, chasing little Eliza across the ice. Or the Marquis de Sade!

So concerned was she with her own anger that she hadn't noticed they had rounded the sharp point of the island and were moving up into a small sandy cove. The boat grounded with a sandpaper noise, thrusting its bow a foot or two beyond the water line.

'Everybody out!' Jake called. Becky looked over the side and grimaced.

'Why do I get the feeling that this is the maiden voyage of the *Titanic*?' she asked querulously. 'Everybody? How darn many people do you think we've got going here?' She drew her knees up into her stomach and stared about her. The island was smaller than she had anticipated, being merely a pine-clad hill. More like Robinson Crusoe than Bermuda, she thought. And her hands bothered her.

'You *are* going to get out?'

Becky jumped. The voice came just inches from her right ear, and it sounded more like 'bed and breakfast' than it did like 'let's play in the sunshine.' She jerked herself awkwardly up from the seat, and almost fell over the side as the craft rocked. Abandoning all dignity she scrambled for the bow and tumbled out on to the beach. On hands and knees, shaking her hair out of her eyes, she glared at him.

'The first one who makes a remark is going to get it,' she muttered. 'Just one remark?'

Jake ignored the challenge. climbing out with all the things she might well have helped carry. And I'm not about to feel guilty about that, she told herself. I hope he trips! And if he offers to help me up I'll—well, I will. She slid back on her haunches, waiting for his next move. He walked right by her.

'There's a little lean-to up on the top,' he told her. 'I'll take this stuff up there. One of them is lunch, isn't it? If not, I'll go back and get the fish.'

'There's lunch in the basket,' she told him firmly. 'And you can forget the fish. I'm not going to cook a fish in this crazy place!'

'And that's for darn sure,' Jake returned. He reached down and picked up a handful of leaves and pine needles from underfoot. 'Look at that.' He ran it from hand to hand in front of her. 'Dry as a bone. Making an open fire here would be like lighting a match to see if your gas tank is full. No fires, lady.'

'Well, in that case, no fish,' she said. Jake smiled down at her and continued up the hill. Damn the man! She was too angry to get up. Damn the man. Some day some poor woman is going to marry him. Think what their children will turn out to be! Tall and lean and devilish—and— why do I let him upset me like that? His children are certainly not going to be mine, so what do *I* care how they turn out!

That little spurt of anger was just enough to clear her

mind. She struggled to her feet, brushed herself down, and plunged into the pinewoods behind him.

He was right when he called it a lean-to. The sides and back seemed strongly built, the roof had obvious deficiences, and its one open side faced towards the east, where a stone fireplace had been built. There was an odour of old fires among the ashes. It flickered on the wind, casting the essence of pine to Becky's nose. There's nothing better than the smell of a wood fire, she told herself.

He came over to stand beside her, and she measured him against the only man she really knew, her stepfather. Solid, this man, but not so wide or so heavily muscled. Not quite as tall as Pop, and skinny. His bones showed everywhere. But that doesn't mean anything, she told herself. Look how much taller I am than Mary Kate! He and I could—damn, what the devil do I care about *that*!

'There's rainwater in that pail behind the lean-to,' he suggested. 'That's as close to antiseptic as we can get. And there's a bar of antiseptic soap beside it. Go and rinse your hands while I spread the lunch.'

'Hey, I'm the doctor,' she muttered under her breath. But she went. Sweet, biddable Rebecca! Huh! If Ma could only see me now!

When she came back around the hut he was stretched out on the grass in front of the lean-to, chomping on the sandwiches she had so hastily made this morning, drinking the lemonade she had so carefully prepared, and having a fine time. It was enough to feed the fires of her anger again, just enough to bring colour to her cheeks and a glare to her eyes. If Jake noticed, he made no comment. She joined him, squirming down near enough to grab at her share of the food. Good manners had been abandoned at the water's edge, she decided.

The air was cool and soothing. The little breeze still played around her head, and the pleasant pungence of the pines filled her nostrils with a heady perfume. She could feel a drowsiness creeping up over her. The world seemed tranquil. She leaned back to study the tops of the trees, swaying against the background of white cotton-wool clouds. Without her volition she was sprawling on her back with her head in his lap. She made an effort to move.

'No, don't do that,' he said softly. 'Relax.' And for no reason that she could understand, Becky did just that. A pair of his fingers came up to trace gentle curls in her hair. The combination of warmth and comfort and security—a moment drawn out of time and held in stasis for their enjoyment—all of it soothed her mind as Jake's busily roaming fingers smoothed her hair, and the world was quiet. She dozed, her mind wandering until his voice called her back.

'You finished medical school?' His voice was soft, cool, interested.

'Yes,' she replied. 'It was a tough struggle, but I made it.'

'You must have been pretty young when you started?'

'Well, I don't know. I finished pre-med in three years, and went into Johns Hopkins when I was twenty-one.'

'So you graduated at twenty-five. Then what?'

'Well, I had to do my internship—but I didn't want it to be the usual rat race. I got approval to do it all in a field hospital established by the American Society of Friends in Chad.'

'That must have been interesting.'

'Medically, yes. First there was starvation, then rebellion, then a Libyan invasion—oh, lord, it was nine months of horror story! And then——' Shut up, she yelled at herself. Tell him your life story, and the next thing you know you'll be featured in one of his raunchy best-sellers!

'And then what?'

'You're not really interested, are you?'

'I really am. Then what?'

'Then we were caught between the government army and the rebels, and we ran out of all sorts of supplies—and then like a fool I forgot to take my Atabrine, and came down with malaria. I didn't mind the bombs, and the artillery, and all that, but that damn mosquito, he knocked me for six. And finally they sent me home. And that's the story of my life. And don't you dare put it in one of your books. Satisfied?'

'Not really,' he chuckled. 'I want to hear the end of the story. Another time?'

'I don't know what you mean.'

'No, of course you don't. Close your eyes.' One of his fingers caressed her eyelids. 'Sleep,' he ordered.

Damned arrogant man! Becky told herself. I'll be darned if I take his orders. But his deep soft voice murmured on, and she did fall asleep.

For a few minutes he stared down at her, all the while twisting curls in her wondrously soft hair. Her lush body, strewn recklessly in sleep, appeared to be abandoned while its owner went off on some other business. Beauty and brains? he asked himself. I've never seen both in one person. Pert, too. I like that. I wonder if her children will look like Michael? And me put *her* in my book? What a laugh that is!

He leaned back against a tree-stump, cast his inhibitions loose, and dropped of into his own wild dreams.

CHAPTER FOUR

IT was the angle of the sun that woke her. As that body moved towards the western cliffs its light and warmth dissipated among the tall pines. Becky felt the heat gradually fade, and forced herself back to life. Not for her the instant response. Like her stepmother, she did poorly for the first hour, and only a mug of coffee could overcome her handicap. She stretched all her muscles, like a cat waking, and tried to sit up. One coil of her hair was trapped in Jake's closed fist, and she twisted around to look. He was sleeping, totally relaxed against the stump, a haunting smile playing at his lips. Without his usual frown, the worry-lines, he looked a thousand years younger, and much more approachable. His grip on her hair was too strong to be broken without waking him up, and she was not quite ready to do that. She turned around again, stretching out with her head in his lap, trying to marshal her thoughts.

She could no longer put off the debate. He had invoked too many strange emotions in her already—and she could not say why. A good-looking man he was not. She had seen hundreds of men easier on the eye than he. Not ugly—not that by any means. In fact, he wore a cloak of easy arrogance, but was a man whom a girl could respect. That was the word. Although she knew nothing about him at all, he was a man who could be respected. And that brings him halfway home, doesn't it? she giggled to herself. Maybe he could develop into a man she could . . . share with, perhaps? Her curiosity bump was too big, too driving, to let her leave it there. She *had* to know. What was Pop's final encomium? Do you like him well enough to share a toothbrush with him? If you do, that's love. But of course, she told herself sombrely, it couldn't be that.

She glanced up into the path of the sun. Good lord, we've left Faith alone too long! she thought. She didn't want to move, but for all her life she had been drilled in responsibility, and it called. But she still could hardly move a muscle until this big ox let loose her hair. Ergo—wake him up!

She grabbed for his nearest arm. Her two hands could hardly span his biceps. She shook him gently, and pain shot up from her blistered hands. A sharp, incisive pain, not to be ignored. But he was moving.

Unlike her, he came awake in an instant. 'Hey, what's this I've caught?' he commented as he lifted up her hank of hair. Becky scrambled to her feet as best she could.

'It's my hair, darn you,' she snapped.

'Why, so it is!' He wants to play cute, she thought. Damn the man!

'Temper, temper!' Jake got himself up and brushed himself off, then he came over behind her and put a hand on each of her shoulders.

'Don't do that! Don't——'

'Don't do what?' There was a a twitch at the corner of his mouth which she could not see.

'Don't—get your hands off me!' she snarled, convinced that he knew what those hands were doing to her.

'Oh—that.' He muttered something under his breath, but she missed it, and dared not ask him to repeat. Be logical, her squirrelling mind told her. Why should you lose control of everything just because he touches you?

'We have to go back,' she said primly, managing to escape from the touch that bothered her so. 'Faith is only nine years old, and we've left her alone for too long. She'll begin to worry.'

'Hah!' he snorted. 'Your sister is nine years old, going on forty. She's a lot older than you are, Becky Latimore.'

'Don't say things like that,' she snapped. 'I love my sister very much, you hear!'

'I hear. You have a heart as big as all outdoors for your own, don't you, little bit? Could you find room for me within the magic circle?'

'How could I?' she asked bitterly. 'I don't know a thing about you, do I? Except that you write. I don't even know *what* you write.'

He had his hands in his pockets again, and she was thankful. As long as they were securely out of the way, they couldn't be torturing her with his touch. She didn't need any more of those wild sensations. She froze her face, giving him the most disdainful look she could muster. It wasn't too shabby an attempt; she had never realised before what a good actress she was.

'All right,' he sighed. 'If information is the price of admission, what is it that you want to know?'

The question had been on the tip of her tongue for days, and it hurried itself out fast enough to embarrass her. 'Are you married?'

'Me? No, I haven't lived the sort of life that leads to marriage.'

'So what kind of life have you lived?'

'I'm an Army brat,' he said as if that explained everything. Becky shrugged her shoulders. It meant nothing to her. Nothing.

'My father was an Army officer,' he said. He was looking away from her, his eyes focused on some infinite distance in space or time. 'My mother and my two sisters and I followed him all over the world. Two years here, three there—never the same place twice. New friends at every move, but never meeting up with the old ones.'

'That sounds interesting. You must have seen a lot of the world. And I'll bet you were close?'

'Yes,' he said, still contemplating the distance. 'Until my father was killed in combat.'

Words failed her. She gave a small gasp of sympathy, and he turned to look at her, dropping an arm over her shoulder. 'I'm not a stray cat,' he said. 'I don't need pity.'

'I wasn't offering it,' she snapped. 'I have a great deal of respect for cats. Then what happened?'

'You can never get rich in the Army,' he said. 'His insurance and his pension took care of Mother and the girls. And I struggled my way through college and followed my father's footsteps.'

'You joined the Army?'

'Yes. They have a fine tuition-assistance programme. They paid my way through . . . graduate programmes. It was after all the wars, I thought. But of course, there never has been an after the wars for us, has there. I ended up in Beirut.'

'Oh, lord!' she exclaimed. 'You weren't in the Embassy when it was blown up?'

'Yes, I was at the Embassy.' His laugh was cold, clipped. 'I was one of the lucky ones. So they gave me a recuperative leave, and I came here to write a book.'

'About Beirut?'

'In a manner of speaking, yes.'

'And then you'll go back in the Army?'

'No. That's all behind me. As soon as my leave is up I'll be resigning. You have something against the Army?'

'No,' she said softly, 'not really. My real father was an Army man. I don't remember him. Ma raised me alone, until she married again, and Pop Latimore adopted me.'

'So being in the military isn't one of the things that prejudices you against me?'

'I'm—I'm not prejudiced against you,' she faltered. 'I—well, perhaps a little. It was some terrible shock to wake up and find myself being thrown in the pool, you know.'

'But you could forgive that, too?'

'I suppose.' Her cheek dimpled. 'Given enough time, and some soothing treatment, I suppose I could.'

'So, now I know where to start,' chuckled Jake, and reached for one of her hands. She backed away from him.

'I only wanted to look at your blisters,' he said. 'I am

definitely not out to rape and pillage.'

'I——' Somehow she was unable to force a sensible word. Instead she held out both hands, palms up. In the soft centre of each a liquid-filled blister trembled.

'Well, it looks as if we need a doctor.' He slipped his hands under hers. She was trembling so much that her arms jumped—but not from pain. No, indeed. 'I guess I can do something about them,' he continued.

'No! Don't break them!'

'Hey, even I know that much,' he said. 'Where is that crazy medical bag of yours?'

'I didn't bring it,' she admitted. 'Well, it isn't a medical trip, for goodness' sakes!'

'I know,' he returned. 'But we need to cover them so you don't accidentally break them open.' He had stripped off his shirt before she could stop him, and his white cotton undershirt followed. 'This is soft enough,' he said as he tore the undershirt into strips.

Becky's eyes were glued on his torso. 'My God!' she exclaimed. The mass of scars started in the middle of his chest and spread in all directions, some still red, newly sewn. His eye followed hers.

'I was buried in the rubble for twenty-four hours,' he explained. 'It took considerable tinkering to put me back together again. Now, don't interrupt.' He made up a little pad from the cotton material, and strapped it on to her palm in a very professional manner. After a moment's study he did the same to the other. Finished, he stepped back to admire the product.

'Looks like an excellent job,' he said. 'You can congratulate me any time you please.'

'Yes, it does, doesn't it,' she offered tentatively. She tested the security of the bandages and watched him at the same time. Her mind was whirling. Writers don't ordinarily apply professional-looking bandages! But then why not? Perhaps he's taken a paramedical course. 'Thank you,' she offered grudgingly through tight lips.

'And very graciously said,' he laughed. 'Oh, my dear Becky, do you always acknowledge help that way? I'm not a Greek bearing gifts, you know. And there are better ways to show your gratitude.'

'Huh!' she snorted. 'I think a kiss is a very expensive return!' And what I need, she told herself, is a great deal more will power, and a considerable injection of common sense!

'I don't feel that way,' he contributed. 'It might be a high price, but what with inflation and all—it's worth it, don't you think?' He stood there smiling, and the sight wrenched at her heart.

'Well, perhaps,' she admitted hesitantly. She moved closer to him. His hands remained at his sides. Very cautiously she moved up against him, extended her arms around his neck, and kissed him gently on the mouth. 'There. Are you satisfied now?'

'Not in the least!' Becky could see the devils peering out of his eyes. Both arms swung around her, pulling her hard against his chest. She was rigid for a moment, and then the world closed in on her, sheltering her in a surprising warmth. His hand gently tilted her chin, and the sky was shut out as his lips came down on hers, gently, teasing.

She relaxed under his hypnotic presence, and the relaxation was her undoing, as his soft caress turned into a wildly victorious assault on all her senses. Furious sensations shot up and down her spine. A rolling wave of fierce passion pushed reason and thought into a dark corner. All she wanted was more. Whatever his passion asked of her, she was prepared to fulfil. And then, just as suddenly, it ended. Jake pushed her away from him, and stepped back.

That quick ending gave her a chance to reassemble herself. Everything except her legs seemed to have returned to normal. But she could not control the trembling in her knees.

'Can you hear that?' he asked.

'What?'

'That noise.'

'It's only an airplane,' she snapped. She had managed to back up against a small pine, and now only her voice was shaking. Lord, if I didn't have enough troubles, she told herself, now I have to go all weak and dreamy over the most arrogant man in the world!

'Thank you,' he offered. She could hear the sarcasm drip off his tongue. 'In case you don't know it, this is a very strange place for an airplane to be flying.' He climbed to the peak of the hill, where a small clearing gave room to look.

'It's a Cessna with pontoons,' he called, and then he came running down the hill, his face alight with expectation. 'Into the boat!' he yelled, dragging her down to the boat with one hand. Before she could find a seat he had pushed the bow off the sandy beach, walked the boat into deeper water, and then vaulted over the stern, sculling them off towards home.

Not a word disturbed their trip. Becky refused to be diverted by a mere flying machine. She sat with her back to it, watching Jake as he applied those tremendous muscles with deceptive power. The scars on his chest danced a macabre waltz as he moved, but he ignored it all. Her mind was troubled. To think of all that punishment, she told herself as her medical eye traced the tormenting scars. And to be almost entombed for a day? There's no limit to this man. And would he ever have told her, had she not seen the scars almost by accident?

Although he was really putting his back into the sculling, his eyes followed the blue and white aircraft as it made one more inspection run over the lake, banked at the north end, and came in for a perfect landing before coasting close to the dock.

His face changed, and she didn't like what she saw.

The look was strange. It seemed to flicker from welcome to disgust, back and forth. It seemed as if a whole new personality was unfolding, but his eyes were not for her. He was following the movement of the aircraft, not too far away now that some detail couldn't be seen. There must be someone on that plane, she told herself, who really turned him on—or off. Maybe both at the same time.

Although she knew she had no claim on him, no right to judge, a pain struck her that was deep and harsh. Rather than continue to watch his face, she swept her feet up over the thwart and reversed her direction.

The aircraft was a private plane, newly painted in cerulean blue and lace white. Its momentum slowed after the landing as the pilot reduced engine speed. It taxied slowly towards the dock. The rowboat was hardly halfway across the lake, and she could feel the boat jump as Jake put his shoulder to the sculling oar.

As the plane closed on the dock, Becky could see someone climbing out of the cabin, to stand on the starboard pontoon. The engine stopped, and the aircraft, out of her environment, waddled like a duck, closer and closer to the dock. The person standing on the pontoon jumped for the wharf, scuffled to secure his balance, then snubbed the rope he was carrying on to the cleat at the dock's edge. Tethered now, the aircraft's forward motion stopped as it crabbed closer to the dock. The cabin door opened again. Suitcases were passed down to the man already on the dock. When a second figure appeared in the cabin door Becky strained her eyes, trying to make out who it might be. Orange sparkled in the distance. It must be a woman, she told herself. Although, God knew, it could be a man in these times.

'Oh, my aching back!' groaned Jake from behind her, and she flashed a look over her shoulder. It wasn't pain that bothered him; it seemed more like disgust.

'It's not who you thought it might be?'

'Hardly,' he groaned. 'I really thought it would be my mother. She said she'd be up to check up on me sooner or later, but——'

'But that's not her?'

'You'd better believe it.' He shrugged his shoulders, as if accepting a gift from an unkind fate. 'Becky,' he said in a very soft voice, 'I need your help.'

'Who, me?'

'Hey, I know you don't like me, Becky, but I need help. That shark who just got out of the airplane is trouble. How about acting as my girl-friend for a few days?

'Who, me?' she repeated. 'I'm not that good an actress!'

'Okay, okay,' he sighed. 'Well, we'll have fun, if nothing else.'

We'll have fun, if nothing else? The words tumbled around in her empty brain. Who's the bigger fool, he or I? Of course, I'd love to *act* as his girl-friend, but my damn pride won't let me! What does he mean, we'll have fun? He and this new one? He and I? He and I and she— whoever she is? Well, I just *don't* like the man, and I certainly don't intend to play the third corner in a triangle. Not me, Buster!

'I wish I could read lips,' he chortled from behind her. 'You are certainly one crazy mixed-up lady, Rebecca.'

'Well, don't get the idea that you're appointed to reform me,' she snarled back at him. 'I like me the way I am!'

'Didn't have much time for men, did you, both at college and medical school?'

She turned around to face him again. 'I'm not the smart one in our family,' she informed him bitterly. 'I——'

'Yes, I know.' His face was solemn, appealing. 'Mattie is the smart one, and she's at M.I.T., right? But look at poor dumb Becky. You finished high school at what, sixteen? College at twenty, and medical school at twenty-five. That's not too shabby, little lady.'

'Don't call me that!' she snapped back at him. 'I'm five foot nine. That's not little!' But the sharp edge of her tongue had worn down under his compliments.

'I call you little because I want to,' he chuckled. 'And don't tell me again that Mattie is the only smart one. You both inherited some brains from somewhere.'

'A lot you know,' she snapped. Why did she want to cry? 'Mattie and I are related only through adoption. Sure I did all those things. I did them by hiding in my room every night, studying until midnight, haunting Pop for explanations. When I—when I went home for vacations from Johns Hopkins I even took my books with me to get help. That's not being smart! Mattie—she works hard, too—but all she has to do is look at a textbook and she can remember everything in it for years and years. She has a photographic memory. Me, all I've got is sweat and tears.'

'So Mattie has a perfect memory! Well, I wish I had one, too. But you have your own thing, Becky. Don't underestimate yourself.' And with that Jake went back to his oar, concentrating on covering distance.

It took another laborious ten minutes before they closed on the dock. In that time the man who had handled the baggage took a long fending pole out of the plane, and gradually the machine was turned around. The outside man scrambled back in, the engine roared, and the little plane taxied back out to the centre of the lake. Its engine revved up a couple of times and it was off, quickly dwindling into the distance. The woman waiting on the dock walked up and down a few times, then sat down on her piled luggage. Her nervous hands lit one cigarette and then another.

They were only a hundred yards out when Jake confirmed Becky's worst suspicions. 'Look at that,' he said in some awe. 'Mavis Pell, queen of Albany society. I can't believe that she . . . I was joking when I invited her up here. I never believed she would come into the woods. Now why the devil couldn't it have been my mother!'

Becky could not resist the chance. 'Mother's boy?'

'I guess,' he admitted wryly. 'You'll see some day. My mother is—I don't know the real word for it— effervescent? She bubbles through life—the same way you do when—oh, lord, me and my big mouth!'

What did he mean? Becky worried the words, like a puppy with a new bone. Effervescent? Me? Or just his mother? And does he like that sort of thing? Or—lord, there are too many "ors" in this world. If I don't watch my Ps and Qs I might even end up liking him! And that's a fate to be avoided.

'Get the bowline,' he broke in on her, and she jerked her head around. The dock was barely ten feet in front of them, and the boat had considerable headway. She stretched, stood up in the boat, and moved forward.

With practised skill, she undid the knot on the little anchor, fletched out the rope, and when he turned the boat at the last minute to run parallel to the dock she stepped off and threw the painter over the nearest bollard. The boat slowed as she applied pressure, and came to rest. He was out over the stern before she could turn around. A fairy wand must have been waved, she thought as she watched, her mouth half open. From grouchy fisherman to Prince Charming!

'Mavis!' he called. 'What a happy surprise!' He held his arms open and the little blonde woman abandoned all her sophisticated pretences and ran to him.

'Oh, Jake,' she cried, 'it's been so long!'

'Well, it won't be long now,' Becky muttered under her breath. 'Oh, Jake—it may never be that long again!' 'Go ahead,' her conscience nagged. 'Be sarcastic! Obviously he thinks a lot of this girl!'

'Sure he does,' she mumbled. 'That's why he propositioned me in the boat, huh?'

'Aw, shut up,' her conscience growled. 'You don't have

to like her, you know. The fact that she's one of those tiny dolls doesn't have to cut any ice with you. Just because she's got a beautiful voice, and probably lights her cigarettes with ten dollar bills, and wears three-hundred-dollar dresses, why should *you* be concerned?'

'Well, she's a long way from civilisation,' she mumbled to herself. 'Wait until she sees the inside of his one-room cabin. Then we'll know, won't we?'

'But what I don't understand,' her conscience nibbled back at her, 'is why are you so insanely jealous about a man you don't even like? Why is that?'

'Oh, shut up,' muttered Becky, and busied herself emptying the boat. She had absolutely no intention of watching that pair kiss each other! She checked out of the corner of her eye to be sure what they were up to. It wouldn't be fair to blame them for something they weren't doing.

She needn't have bothered. They were doing just what she suspected, and it lasted for ever and ever. She turned away in disgust. Right out in public. You'd think they had no shame!

'To hell with both of them,' she muttered as she smashed the fishing tackle down on the dock. 'To hell with everybody!' The poor dead fish, the only occupant left, glared up at her. 'And to hell with you, too,' she muttered as she stalked away from the boat, down the dock.

She stopped once and turned to watch them. They were still playing the snuggling bit. She shrugged her shoulders in disgust and started up the trail towards the house. Halfway up she met Faith coming down.

'I heard the airplane, but I was in the bath,' her sister explained. 'Is something interesting going on?'

'Hardly,' Becky said disgustedly. 'His girl-friend has just arrived.'

'You mean she's right here?' Faith was getting excited, and when she did her eyes lit up like searchlights. 'I'll bet she's a famous movie star or something!'

'Probably. They're down at the dock,' Becky sighed. 'I left everything down there. Would you mind bringing some of it up while I do something about my blisters?'

'Would I! To see a movie queen! Thanks, Becky!'

'Thanks? Thanks for what,' muttered Becky, watching Faith dash off down the trail. 'I'll bet she's something else besides a a movie queen!' 'Meow!' Becky's conscience interrupted. 'Sour grapes!'

'Mind your own business!' Becky Latimore shouted at the world. She walked into the kitchen on tiptoe. And that bothered her, when she thought of it. After yelling all over the globe outside, you have to pussyfoot inside? What sort of logic is that? she asked herself.

'Damn the logic,' she muttered, and switched on the gas under the coffee pot. She was on her second cup when she heard voices coming up the hill, but she refused to get up, even though she was eager to know who it was. There was no noise at the front door. She glued her eyes in that direction. So when the screen door of the patio slid open behind her she jumped and spilled all her coffee over the floor. 'Damn! Damn!' She sang it like a litany. 'Now look what you've done!'

'Who, me?' Faith was in her usual bubbling good humour. 'I didn't do it, but I *will* clean it up.' She was into the cupboard under the sink and came out with a cleaning sponge. In the meantime Jake Meadows and his guest had followed her into the house. He was all smiles.

'Becky,' he said genially, 'I'd like you to meet Mavis Pell, an old friend of mine.'

Becky stepped forward. Too many years of drill under her mother's eagle eye made it impossible for her to be impolite. She manufactured a smile, extended her hand, and hoped that no one would notice how much she was shaking.

'I'm pleased to welcome you to Lake Mohawk.' The other woman took the proffered hand, agitated it slightly, and let it go.

'A pleasure,' Mavis murmured. It obviously wasn't true, but Becky was in no mind to make an issue of it. Instead, she held her tongue and really looked. Five foot two, or thereabouts. Short enough to make Becky self-conscious. Beautiful blonde hair. It looked real, almost down to its roots. Blue eyes—of course. Damn that Scandinavian blood! Lovely figure, with more emphasis than necessary on what American men admire most. Damn! I'll bet she plays the organ and sings in the church choir as well. And on alternate weekends goes around do-gooding!

'I've got all that mess cleaned up,' Faith, from just behind her, announced triumphantly. 'I went into Mr Meadows' cabin, Becky, and you know what I thought?'

What she wanted to shout was 'No, I don't, and I don't want you to tell me!' But it came out, 'No, but I suppose you're going to tell me?'

'Oh, you are funny,' her sister laughed. 'Isn't she, Jake?'

'I don't think this is the place for me to say a single word,' he returned.

'You—*you're* going to tell me, Faith?'

'Yup. We went into Jake's cabin, and you know it's only got one room. He has two bunks in it, one for himself and the other covered with his book stuff, and Mavis has come to help him with his book, only there's no way she could stay down there, and that's why I did it.' Faith took a deep breath, turned on her nicest smile, and shrugged her shoulders in that almost-Gallic way she had inherited from Ma.

'Did what, love?' Becky found it to be a particular strain, getting that many words through frozen lips. Luckily, there was a loud noise in the dining room as the two-way radio cleared its throat and began calling.

'That's for us!' shrieked Faith. 'I'll get it!' She dashed for the door, stopping only long enough to look over her shoulder. 'That's why I invited Miss Pell to stay up here with us!' Before Becky could protest, the door slammed shut between them.

There was an awkward silence in the kitchen. Jake Meadows and his new-found helper moved closer together. He put one protective arm around the woman, and they both stared at Becky.

She moistened her dry lips, and hid her hands behind her back, where they could shiver and twist to their hearts' content. 'Yes,' she said cautiously, 'you certainly are welcome.'

Her words broke the still-life in scattered parts. Becky found that her eyes just wouldn't focus. Everything within the kitchen seemed blurred. She turned around to hide the tears.

'This will be a wonderful help to me,' Jake was saying. In her condition it seemed to Becky as if he were talking down an empty barrel. 'She'll be so close, and it will be so convenient, and——'

Whatever he was saying just drifted in and out of Becky's mind. '—able to work every day——' She gave up, letting it all soar out into the sunlight. By disconnecting her ears she could stand there and watch his lips move, and . . . they were both staring at her again. She brought herself back to the present with a snap.

'Well, whatever else, it will be close for you both,' she said weakly. 'Do you want me to walk down and help with the luggage?'

'No need of that,' he returned. 'We brought it all up with us.'

'Everything?'

'Including that darn fish!'

'Lord, I—come on, Miss Pell, let me show you to a room. I'm sure you must be tired from the trip.'

'I'll bring the suitcases,' Jake added.

The little blonde bombshell had nothing to say. Becky swallowed, indicated the direction of the stairs, and

started off ahead. Maybe that's the trick, she told herself.
Blondie has spoken a total of three words so far, and here
she is, Queen of the Hill! Damn! She had slapped at the
banister, and her palm was letting her know that the
blisters were still there. She trudged to the top of the
stairs, one hand raised at her breast, the other gently
holding it at the wrist.

'I'll put you in Mother's room,' she said, throwing the
door open. Mavis followed close on her heels, moving
around the room to check the view, running a finger
across the undusted bureau, testing the tension of the
bedsprings. But all she had to say was, 'Is there a
bathroom?'

'There.' Becky pointed to the door in the opposite wall.
The newcomer got up from the bed and stretched. Lord,
that's strictly for masculine consumption, Becky told
herself. She's wasting it on me.

But, of course, Miss Mavis Pell didn't intend to waste a
good stretch on another female. Jake was at the door,
loaded down with suitcases, and looking suitably
impressed. Having made her mark, Mavis strolled across
to the bathroom and walked in for inspection. I feel like
an inn-keeper, Becky told herself. Should I run after her
and take notes? I'll say one thing—or rather two things
about this vacation. I should get plenty of practice
hating. Arrogant Jake and his Despicable Doxie. Wow,
wouldn't that make a great novel?

Steps clattered and Faith stuck her head in the door.
'Daddy!' she screamed. 'It's Daddy! He wants to talk to
you on the radio. Hurry up, Becky!'

'Ah, the Commander calls?' Jake wore an ear-to-ear
grin. Mavis came out of the bathroom, drying the tips of
her fingers on a guest towel. And how that got in there I'll
never know, Becky told herself. I thought I'd taken
everything——

'It's perhaps a little—well, of course it will do, darling,'
Miss Pell said as she walked over and slipped a

proprietorial arm under his elbow. 'I came mentally prepared to suffer some discomfort. I'd do this and more for you!' He squeezed her hand and looked down at her as if blonde were truly the only way of life.

'Becky!' Faith was yelling from the foot of the stairs. 'Pop says right now——'

'I'm coming, I'm coming!' Becky roared back as she moved towards the door. Jake followed her.

'This is a wonderful thing you're doing,' he whispered in her ear.

'Yes, isn't it?' she responded stiffly.

'Becky!' the roar came from downstairs again. 'Pop says—you'd better hurry.'

'Yes, of course. Hurry! It's all my fault,' Becky muttered under her breath as she went down the stairs two at a time. 'I'm guilty of everything. Including giving lodgings under false pretences.'

'What did you say?' Faith had never seen her sister in such a mood, and stood waiting for her at the foot of the stairs. 'You don't look so good!'

'So now you're a doctor, too,' she snarled, and instantly regretted it. 'No, I didn't mean that.' She dropped a loving hand on her sister's shoulder. 'That was the devil speaking, love. You go and check on Her Majesty, while I talk to Pop. Okay?'

'Okay. You'd better hurry!'

And hurry she did, remembering to close both the dining-room doors behind her. She sat down at the little table in the far corner, picked up the microphone, and pushed the 'talk' button. 'Pop?' There was just the tremble of a tear in her voice.

The radio cleared its throat. 'Becky, love.' There was a wealth of loving behind that deep voice. Just two words, and he had lifted a great weight from her shoulders. She need not be a beginning medical doctor, standing on reputation and experience. She needed only to be the eldest daughter of a man whose shoulders were broad enough for her problems and for everyone else in the family who had troubles.

'Oh, Pop,' she cried into the microphone, 'I'm being such a darn fool!'

CHAPTER FIVE

BY the end of the second week Becky had come to the end of her patience. As she sat over her early morning coffee, grown cold by the delay, she debated for the twentieth time the polite way to rid the house of termites. Well, one termite by the name of Mavis Pell. It had all seemed so inevitable. First of all there was Faith, the sister who lived up to her name. Faith had invited Mavis to live with them, and left Becky with no room to manoeuvre. And then there had been her talk with her father by radio.

After the usual exchanges between two people who loved each other dearly, and considerable soothing, her father had said, 'Now, if all you people are happy out in the Berkshires, I think I shall kidnap your mother and take her to Bermuda. She's not required to sit on the Bench until October, and when she starts that I'm afraid she'll wear herself to the bone. So—all of you will be okay? What about this man your mother referred to?'

She wanted desperately to say, 'Pop, please come and get us as quickly as you can.' But she remembered the wan look on her mother's face as she packed the bags, set the house in 'proper motion' and dealt with Michael's little hurts. And how that face had lit up at the thought of a childless vacation. And you're the eldest daughter, she told herself. You're the assistant mother. She forced a smile into her voice.

'You mean Mr Meadows? Well, he hasn't been much of a bother, you know. He hurt his hand—with a fish-hook—and after I sewed him up we sort of entered into a neutrality pact. Michael thinks he's grand. So does Faith—with some reservations.'

77

'Come on now, little girl, it's your father you're talking to, not some back fence neighbour. Give it to me straight!'

'Well, they both do!'

'You know what a terrible judge of character Michael is. Speak up, girl!'

'I——' and then the tears broke through. 'He's a terribly arrogant, opinionated—well, perhaps not that bad, but almost. And I don't like him worth a nickel. Would you believe that?'

'Not really. What's the rest of the story?'

'He—well—he brought this girl with him. Her name is Mavis Pell. And I—Faith invited the girl to stay here with us—and I go around trying to figure a way to push her down the stairs, or pull her hair out, or something. You wouldn't know about that!'

'Oh yes, I would,' he laughed. 'I had the same trouble with your mother, but I kept after her, and I'm glad I did.'

'Oh, Daddy,' Becky sighed, 'I wish I could be as lucky as you and Mom. We'll be okay. I can stand it until the summer's over. And, Daddy?'

'What is it, honey?'

'I want to thank you for all the loving you've given me—even though I'm not one of your own.'

There was a short silence on the circuit. 'Hey, Becky! Don't you know what that means? All the others just came along. We love them, you must know that, but they just came along. Now you, Rebecca, we *chose* you! It makes a mite of difference. You are our *first* love—don't forget that. Now, if you can handle things, I'm going to take your mother on that trip. She's very tired. And while I'm gone, our Mr Riley will be in charge.'

'Ooooh! Uncle Charlie!'

'Yes, you and he have always had a thing going between you, haven't you?' She could hear the laughter in his voice.

'Ever since you and Ma went off on your honeymoon. I told Uncle Charlie that I thought *nobody* would ever marry *me*, because I was too big and clumsy.'

'And?'

'And he told me—very solemnly too—that if I were not married by the time I was thirty-five, he'd marry me himself! My first proposal, Pop. Come to think of it, my *only* proposal!'

'Well, you're in luck, lovely lady. Your Uncle Charlie keeps talking about retiring, but he'll be here, available by radio. Now, scoot out of there, love, and give that Mavis Whatchamacallit a hard time!'

And now, Becky told herself as she swirled the coffee mug, I've run out of steam. Lady Bountiful, this woman thinks she is. Can you imagine that!

'Any of that coffee left?' Faith ghosted in, absolutely silent in her fur slippers and light nightgown. Her long blonde hair was in a tangled mess, and there were frown lines on her young face.

'No, even I can't drink this stuff,' Becky returned. And then, in a burst of energy, 'But you never drink coffee. It's always orange juice or milk.'

'I know,' her sister sighed, 'but today I need coffee. It's a stimulant, isn't it?'

'Okay, okay,' laughed Becky. 'One fresh cup of coffee coming up. And what makes *you* so gloomy this early in the morning?'

'It can't be the weather, can it?' Faith wandered hopefully over to the kitchen window. The sun was late peaking over the hills, but it was definitely coming. 'We haven't had rain for over a month, have we?'

'More likely three. It's been the longest dry spell in this century, according to the radio news. But it's not the weather that's got to you, is it?'

'No, it's not,' her younger sister snapped. Faith showing bad humour was about as likely as the Red Sox winning the baseball pennant. Becky walked around the table and put a hand on her shoulder.

'So, tell me,' she invited.

'I hate being a servant in my own home,' the child said. 'What *is* it with that woman? Can't be out of bed until after ten in the morning, has to have her breakfast in bed, must have her clothes laundered every day—but can't do it for herself. Can't eat what the common people eat. My Gawd!'

'Funny thing,' murmured Becky, 'I couldn't have said it better myself. But as from today the war begins.'

'War? What war?'

'The revolution of the Latimore women, that's what. Get yourself ready for a day on the lake while I make a packet of sandwiches. This time, when ten o'clock rolls around, little Cinderella up there is going to find herself in an empty house. Up, up, and away!'

They took the canoe, it being easier to manoeuvre in the more narrow parts of the lake. Becky knelt in the bow to provide the power, while Faith squatted in the stern to steer. The morning passed quickly, full of the quiet little gems of pleasure that one stumbles upon of a summer morning. They lunched at Three Pine Island, took naps together, then slowly headed for the home dock.

All told, they beached the canoe at about two in the afternoon, and, still highly conversational, rambled up the hill. That man was out in his front yard, chopping wood.

'Hey!' Becky protested. He stopped, wiped his forhead on a big red bandana, and sat down on the stump he had been using for a chopping block.

'Ah, the Latimores have come among us,' he saluted.

'Ah, your doctor has come among you,' snapped Becky. 'Let me see that hand!'

He grinned, but obeyed, standing in front of her like some schoolboy about to be told his faults. 'Well, give me the hand!' He extended his hand. The bandage was soiled and torn. Damn the man, Becky told herself, look what he's doing! She stripped the tape which bound the compress to the wound. He muttered a couple of words as she pulled at the hairs on his wrist. The little cut, long since missing its stitches, looked as good as one might expect, but to chop wood? Her conscience could not permit that.

'It looks good, but you shouldnt use it to hold an axe,' she told him, mustering her best hospital voice. 'Come up to the house and let me put a fresh bandage on it.'

'And how do I get the wood cut for the fire? It's mighty chilly around these parts at two in the morning.'

'You should get Miss Pell to help out,' Becky suggested sarcastically. 'She's not all that busy, you know.'

He looked down at her in surprise. 'Why, I do believe you don't like Mavis,' he said sorrowfully.

If I weren't barefoot, Becky promised herself, I'd kick him right in that big ugly shin of his. Don't like Mavis? That's putting it mildly!

'You're talking to yourself again,' he chuckled.

'Come on, Becky, we'd better get up to the house,' Faith seized her sister's hand and tried to drag her away.

'Just a minute,' Becky said. 'I have another word or two I want to say to Mr Meadows here.'

Faith tugged again, with no success, then looked over her shoulder at Jake.

'You know, you're a great disappointment to me,' she told him. There was more dignity in her voice than her nine years could provide.

'Me?'

'You. Come on, Becky.'

For some unexplainable reason Becky wanted to stay just where she was. Faith shrugged and headed up the hill.

'How are the mighty fallen,' he quoted sombrely. 'But it's only a misunderstanding. I'll straighten it all out later.'

'Don't count on it,' Becky snapped. 'She's easily

swayed, but I'm going to bake her an apple pie this afternoon that will make her head spin! She's on *my* side. Don't cut wood with that hand. How *is* Miss Pell, for that matter?'

'Miss Pell isn't feeling too well,' he returned. 'That was a dirty trick, Becky.'

'What? Making her own breakfast? Or was it the shock of having to get out of bed to eat it?'

'Now, if that isn't just like a woman! Sarcasm and envy all rolled up in a neat package. You just don't like Mavis, do you?'

'She's a guest in my house,' Becky snapped. 'I don't have to like her. My sister invited her to stay, and she's staying. She treats it like a hotel. And come to think of it, just what does Miss Pell do for a living?'

'A living? Work? You must surely know that Mr Gideon Pell owns most of the land that the city of Albany sits on?'

'Like that, huh? Dear old Daddy takes care of little Mavis, does he?'

'Now, now, Becky! She can't help being born rich. Just because you come from a poor family—hey, wait a minute. Helicopters, jeeps—Latimore. Your father isn't *that* Latimore, is he? The biggest construction company in the United States?'

'Yes,' she returned through gritted teeth. 'And we all have to work. Always have. My dad made all his money by hard work, not sitting on his——'

'Now, now, Becky, watch the language!'

'Huh! Well, a lot you know, Mr Meadows. A lot you know! And just what is little Miss Richwitch doing now?'

'She's—ah—helping me with my book, if you must know.'

'I don't hear anything. Is she a typist?'

'Well—not exactly. But she *is* trying.'

'You'd do better with a typist. You don't look like

a man who needs people standing around being supportive!'

'Now that's the nicest thing you've said to me all week,' he chuckled. 'To tell the truth, the book is hung up in its last chapter, and Miss Pell has gone back up the hill to rest before dinner. What are you having?'

'Pork chops and mashed potatoes. Peas for decoration.'

'My, that sounds good. Faith won't eat peas?'

'Nothing that's green. She claims there are worms in green vegetables. What are *you* having for supper?'

'Worms,' he sighed. 'I'm not much of a cook.'

And there she was, backed into a trap of her own making. Her face flushed and her eyes flashed, but there was no way to evade what good manners dictated. 'Why don't you come and have dinner with us?' she said disgustedly.

'What a kindhearted person you are!' Jake chortled. He moved closer to her, until they stood almost toe to toe. Desperate orders channelled from her brain to her feet. 'Move!' The feet refused. His arms came around her trembling shoulders. One of his fingers toyed with her hair, moved down to her chin and elevated it. Those sea-dark eyes of his seemed so huge, so deep, and she was drowning in them. His other arm tightened around her, pressing her close against the steel wall of his chest. His head came down towards her. Becky closed her eyes and shivered. Nothing seemed to happen.

She forced one eye open. As if he had been waiting for the signal, his lips came down on hers, warm and moist and sweet, barely touching, but delivering his message none the less. She fell into the trap. She wanted more. She stretched up on tiptoe, forcing herself against him, wanting more—of whatever it was. More of that something that made her long to surrender herself entirely to his keeping. All that from just the slightest kiss. Soon begun, sooner ended. Jake gripped her by the forearms and set her away from him.

She shook her head, sending her long black hair forward around her face in a raven-dark mask. 'None of that,' he said quietly, brushing the hair aside with one finger. 'Poor Becky Latimore! All those years of studying in a medical convent, and now you're out in the real world. What do you think, Becky?'

She managed to clamp down on her emotions, but could not face those eyes. With bowed head, 'Think about what?' she murmured. 'I don't know what you're talking about.'

She wrenched herself out of his grip and ran up the path as if all the hounds of Hell were after her. While Jake just stood where he was and laughed.

Dinner was early that night. When Becky puffed up to the house, both Faith and Mavis were gathering at the swimming pool, circling each other like a pair of unfriendly cats.

'Could we eat early tonight?' The blonde Miss Pell had that sort of high sweet voice that one noticed immediately.

'Five o'clock do?' Becky was willing to compromise. After all, the woman *was* a guest in her home.

'Yes, certainly.' Mavis smiled then, a secretive smile that promised much but said nothing. And so, after a dip in the pool to wash away the early part of the day, Becky went off to the kitchen. In a short time her sister Faith joined her. 'Set an extra place,' Becky called from the kitchen. 'Mr Meadows is going to join us.'

'Well, now, isn't that a surprise,' giggled Faith. 'Shall I put out an extra glass? You *are* going to poison him, aren't you?'

'Not tonight, love. I think we'll let him live a little longer. Not much longer, perhaps.'

Mavis came in from the pool at four-thirty, looked at the clock, and ran for her room.

'Are we to be blessed with fancy dress tonight?' Faith

had come out to the kitchen, speaking in whispers.

'Maybe,' Becky returned. 'I've got all this in hand now. Why don't you scoot and get your shower? It wouldn't hurt, either, to dress up. You know Ma always likes that.'

'Okay,' Faith returned, 'but will you look at what's coming up the path!' Becky took a quick peep. Jake Meadows, of course, dressed to kill. Dark trousers, a white dinner jacket, white shirt, and bow tie. 'Fit to kill,' Becky confirmed as she moved away from the window. 'All right, now, Faith. Scoot!' She added an affectionate pat as the little girl grinned at her and raced up the stairs. Jake came in through the kitchen door without knocking.

'Smells nice,' he offered. 'Mighty nice.'

'It's nothing difficult to make,' she returned, feeling as if he had just tendered her an olive branch.

'Don't underestimate yourself,' he said solemnly. 'There are always enough people around to run you down. You shouldn't add to it yourself.'

'Confucius says?'

'Nope. That's from the third book of Jake Meadows. Can I help?'

'I don't think so. Everything is about ready. Faith just ran upstairs to dress. If you'll excuse me, I'd better snatch a minute or two for the same. There's a bar-cabinet in the dining room. Help yourself.'

'Don't mind if I do,' he drawled. 'Say, I did enjoy— talking to you this afternoon. We must do that again some time.'

'I doubt it very much,' she retorted, with as much acid in the words as she could assemble.

'Brr!' He wrapped his arms around himself as if to protect from the cold. 'I never knew a cold front to come in so fast. What happened?'

She gave him one slow solemn stare, then turned her back on him and walked gracefully up the stairs. All the while she could feel his eyes boring into her back, following every swaying motion. It was hard not to start running. She managed to maintain control up to the door of her own room. Safe inside she collapsed on the bed, undecided. Should I laugh or cry? she asked herself. Her little wall clock sounded the quarter-hour. She did neither. There was no time for a shower. She quickly stripped, slipped into fresh underwear, drew her favourite light ivory dress over her head, smoothed it all down, and looked in the mirror. Her hair was a mess. Wind and water had triumphed. She reached for a hairbrush, just as the kitchen timers went off.

'Oh, lord,' she muttered. 'What a choice to make! Either look like a windblown tramp or burn the dinner?' The dinner won. She snatched up her hairbrush and took it with her as she went down the stairs, two at a time.

Faith was already at work in the dining-room. Becky took one quick look, then ducked into the kitchen. Jake was there, pulling her pies out of the oven, looking as if it were something he did every day. Sure he does, she told herself sarcastically.

'Good-looking,' he commented, setting the last pie down on the cooling rack.

'The pies?' she asked cautiously.

'No, you.' Before she could put the table between them he was in front of her, holding her firmly in position by his grip on her forearms. 'Good enough to eat,' he announced.

'For heaven's sake, get your hands off me!' she snarled at him. 'What the devil do you think I am, the first course?'

'Delightfully waspish sense of humour,' he chuckled. 'I appreciate that in a woman. But don't let it go too far. It could interfere with our enjoyment of other things.'

'Like what?' snapped Becky, and immediately regretted having made a sound.

'Like this.' Jake pulled her forward against him. She struggled for a second, but the moment his arms closed around her she lost all interest in fighting him off. It wasn't that her subconscious mind was not sending alarm signals, but rather that, having received the alarms, her body just didn't seem to care! I won't do that, she muttered into his shirt. But her arms crept up and around his neck, and by the time his lips touched hers, she was providing a considerable part of the physical power that locked them together. She closed her eyes and let her sensations run rampant. Until someone behind them breezed through the door, took a look, and said very loudly, 'Excuse me, I didn't realise this was a private affair.' Faith was giggling as she closed the door again.

At the first words Jake started to break off the contact. It was not wholly successful. His arms were certainly moving her backward, but his lips refused to break the contact. Suddenly she was free.

She found it hard to breathe. It was almost as if she had run a twenty-six-mile marathon. She glanced quickly up at him. He was having breathing trouble, too. Good for you! she muttered under her breath. Once again her hair was all over her face, hiding the brilliant blush of red that stained her cheeks. She needed help standing up. One of the old high-backed kitchen chairs was near at hand. She put out one fumbling hand, took a grip, and relaxed.

'Mr Meadows,' she spluttered, 'this—this attack business has got to stop! If your Miss Pell can't satisfy your needs, I recommend that you import somebody else!'

'Why should I do that when I have you?' She flashed another look at him. He appeared to be serious!

'Well, that's the whole point, isn't it? You *don't* have me. I don't want to be had—at least not by you. Now, will you kindly go out to the dining-room and leave me to finish up? Faith will be wanting some sort of explanation. You might try to think up a good excuse while you're at it.'

'Yes, ma'am.' He offered her a strained grim look,

bowed a stiff Germanic bow, and went through the door.

'What in the world does he think he wants?' Becky muttered as she pulled the vegetables off the stove, then strained and dished them. Then to the oven again. The chops were done to a turn. She fumbled for a hot pad, took them out, then set them on the waiting platter. The task was simple, but complicated by her string of muttered comments—all about him, of course. She took out her rage on the potatoes, mashing and smashing at them until nothing could be seen of their original form. By the time she had the dishes prepared, Faith came in.

'Lady Bountiful is among us,' the younger girl giggled. 'She's having a cocktail with Jake.'

'From now on in this house he's Mr Meadows,' snarled Becky, and was instantly sorry. Why take it out on Faith?

'Yeah. I could see him being Mr Meadows,' her sister returned, not at all squelched by Becky's tone of voice. 'A couple more minutes of that, I would have been tempted.'

'Don't be so nosey!' But Becky was unable to leave well enough alone. 'Tempted to do what?'

'Well, I wasn't sure.' The girl cleared a space on the table and rested a hip on it. 'I wasn't sure whether to get on the radio and call Pop, or just go upstairs for the shotgun and settle it all right here and now!' At which point she broke out into such a mad flight of giggles that they bent her over.

'Yes, well, I'm glad *somebody* finds it all humorous. I certainly didn't.'

'No, of course not. I could see you weren't enjoying a minute of it.'

'Don't be sarcastic. Take the vegetabes and potatoes through!' Faith studied her sister's face, finally seeing the hurt, the humiliation in it all. She said not another word, but picked up the plates and went into the dining room.

By the time Becky had finished arranging the chops and setting out the apple sauce, she had calmed down.

Somewhat, that was. She took the platter into the dining-room, where everyone else was waiting.

There seemed to be a little black raincloud poised over that meal. Conversation was thin on the ground, and Faith was in active rebellion.

'Eat your peas!' Becky finally hissed at her.

'No!' Seeing nothing but battle ahead, Becky surrended. The offending peas were whipped out of the way, and apple pie was substituted.

'It's been a charming meal,' Mavis exclaimed as Jake assisted her with her chair. 'I don't know when I've had more fun, but Jake and I have a party to go to. Such lovely conversation! I do think that children under fifteen should eat separately.'

'I don't agree,' snapped Becky, unwilling to have outsiders attack a family member. 'We have to make allowances. Surely you've noticed that in your own family?'

'Heavens, no, my dear. I'm an only child, you know.' And with that, plus a fluttery little wave of the hand, Mavis was gone. Jake gave them all a big grin, and went along after her.

'That only goes to prove what I told Hope,' Faith said glumly. Becky was busy clearing the table, pinching an occasional bit off the end of the left-over chops.

'What was that?'

'I told her that Jake—I mean Mr Meadows— wasn't the right one for us!'

'Oh, did you? The right one for what?'

'The right one for us to get you married off, Becky.' There was a tremendous nine-year-old sigh to accompany the statement.

'You don't have to wait for me in order to get married yourself, love. You can go right ahead and do it whenever you want to. But don't you think that you're a little early for that sort of thing?'

'No, I don't think so,' her sister commented. 'I've

asked around. Everybody I've talked to said you was gonna be an old maid. And when I got so mad at Jake— at Mr Meadows—I told him he just wouldn't do, 'cause you would rather be an old maid than marry a guy like him!'

'You *what*?'

'I told Mr Meadows. The day after he come up here and threw you in the swimming pool. He wasn't supposed to do that, and it made me mad. So I told him all about it.'

'You actually—told *that man* about me?'

'Why, yes, Becky. I told him we didn't need him, 'cause you had plenty of boy-friends, and maybe you didn't really wanna get married anyway. What's wrong with that, Becky?'

It was a little too much. Becky felt that her head weighed five thousand pounds. She pushed the dishes aside and made a place to rest her head. He knew all about—that—it would be like waving a red flag in front of a bull! Is that why he kept nipping after me? Oh, God!

'Did I say something wrong, Becky?'

'No, no—not really. I——' She lifted her head up and used a knuckle to clear the drops of moisture from her eyes. 'No, not really, pet. Let's get these dishes out of the way and things are bound to be brighter.'

CHAPTER SIX

BECKY heard him as he came around the house to the kitchen door. She was rolling pie-dough again. It had been left over from her last batch of pies, and she had frozen it. There were plenty of apples still available, and, with a little more effort, she proposed to present the pies as her apologies for stupidly losing her temper. The door was open, but the screen door was closed. Jake knocked and came in at her call. He appeared hesitant, as if not sure of his welcome.

'Well, look at that,' he said. 'I surely did enjoy the pie the other night. I surely did.'

Becky looked up at him quickly, and then back down to her work. Too much staring leads to strange thoughts, she told herself. Especially with *this* man. 'Time must hang heavily on your hands,' she responded quietly. 'It was only last night that we ate the pies.'

'Only—good lord, so it was! It really seems like a couple of months ago.'

She reached for her roller and began to press out the crust, using more energy than it required—by a long shot. 'Your—partner.' Her nose was itching, and she dared not rub it, not with her hands covered with flour. 'Your associate hasn't honoured us at all today. She said something about a headache, took four aspirins, and crawled back to bed.'

'I bet she did,' he said mournfully. 'It was a terrible night. We drove all the way to Pittsfield, and found most of the town shut down when we got there. Why are you wiggling your nose that way?'

'It itches,' she snapped. 'And I can't scratch it until my hands are clean.'

91

'Hold still.' He came close to her—closer than she felt necessary—or safe. One of his hands—the damaged one— came up to her nose level, and with one finger he gently rubbed the end of her nose. 'Right there?'

'Ah—no—not quite. Just a little bit higher.' There was something erotic to all this. She fought against the impulse to say—or do—something foolish. His finger moved up the bridge of her nose, busily rubbing it all the way. 'Like that?'

'Oh, that's just fine,' she sighed, and started to back away from him. His hands came down on her shoulders and halted the retreat. 'What—what do you want?'

'I don't really know,' he said. 'How about this?' He bent down and kissed the tip of her nose, right at the heart of its problem.

Becky was startled by the whole, and yet strangely attracted to his gentleness. But there was the feeling that he was too close.

'You'll get flour all over you,' she told him, reaching desperately for an excuse. The threat failed to impress him. They both heard footsteps on the stairs. She could see his eyes light up, as if someone had pulled a switch.

'Now what the devil are you up to?' she started to say. But just as she got to the 'devil' part of it Jake had pulled her close again, bent his head quickly to hers, and sealed her off from the world by a warm moist kiss. The touch of his lips was a comfort that gradually turned into something else as his arms pressed her closer. Becky struggled for a second, then gave up all resistance as a firestorm of emotion swept over her. It was not because she hadn't the strength to fight back, but more because she wanted to join in. Her hands were trembling, shaking, with no place to go. She hesitated, then sent them stealing up and around his neck, clasping them together at his nape, peppering his hair with a spurt of white flour. Neither noticed; they were both bound up in the surprising swirl of feelings that encompassed them unexpectedly. Neither heard the kitchen door open. Both heard the squall of indignation from Mavis Pell.

'What in hell is going on here!' Anger propelled the blonde across the kitchen to their side. But the hopelessly entwined pair paid no attention. Mavis grabbed Jake by the arm and shook it, and the message finally arrived. He slowly broke contact with Becky, tucking her head up under his chin as he did so. At least he had some breath to respond with. Becky had none. She gasped desperately for air, for a halt to this mindless turmoil that held her in thrall.

'What the hell's going on here?' Mavis repeated.

'It seems fairly obvious,' he drawled. But he hadn't gone unscathed, Becky noted. There was a slight quaver in his usually smooth voice, and a line of perspiration across his forehead. 'Anyone can see that I'm kissing the cook,' he continued, 'and making a good job of it until now. Did anyone ever tell you, Mavis, that you've got a terrible sense of timing?'

The blonde nibbled on her lip for a second, then decided to play it all in low key. 'Taking samples, are you, darling? Do you want me to go out and make a noise before I come in again?'

Kissing the cook? The phrase shook Becky to her senses—raging, boiling senses. 'You don't need to do that,' she said coldly. 'If this is some sort of game they play in your society, please excuse me. I don't care to play sex games!'

'That wasn't a game,' Jake offered mildly.

'You're in over your head,' the other woman said simultaneously.

'Maybe you're both right,' Becky stormed. 'I would appreciate it if you would both get out of my kitchen. And the quicker the better!'

'Now that's clear-cut enough,' Mavis told him, laying a hand on his arm. 'Why don't we go outside? Too many cooks spoil the dinner, or something like that.'

He shrugged her arm off. 'I'm here to help the lady,' he said. 'Nobody else seems to. What can I do, Becky?'

'Nothing,' she said woodenly. 'Everything's been done—and——'

'And you wouldn't want my help if I were the last man on earth?' A grim uncompromising statement, that dug little holes in her heart. She balled up her fists and beat on his chest.

'I told you in the boat,' she cried, 'that I wouldn't—that I——'

'I do believe I'll go out on the patio,' Mavis interrupted. 'It's ever so much cooler out there.' With her fists suspended in mid-air Becky stared at the woman's back as she swayed through the screen door and clopped around to the other end of the pool.

'You told me what?' Jake had both her wrists trapped in his hands, pressing hard enough to bring pain.

'I told you that I wouldn't be a decoy for you and your little society pigeon!' she roared, 'and I won't. You hear me? I won't!'

'I wasn't playing a game, Becky,' he said solemnly. He gently lowered her arms to her sides and let them go. Oh, God, she cried to herself, if I could only believe him. What have I done!

He was leaning against the refrigerator, watching her, seeing clearly the terrible internal war she was fighting. He offered the olive branch again. 'Can I help with the supper?'

'I—no——' she stuttered. 'We're having pizza. It's almost all ready for the oven.'

'I love pizza. Especially home-made.' The olive branch again. Becky accepted it eagerly.

'Would you—stay for supper?'

'For ever, if I ever get invited,' he returned, laughing. He stood away from the refrigerator and moved in her direction. She flinched and backed off.

'You've got flour in your hair,' she told him primly.

'All right,' he said quietly. 'I'll be out on the patio, too. But don't forget, Becky, you and I have to talk after dinner.'

'We do?' She fumbled in her strained mind for some idea what he was talking about, but managed not an item. She stood by the kitchen table, her flour-encrusted hands thrust into the pockets of her apron, and watched as he went out of the back door.

That last conversation bothered her all through dinner. We have to talk? About what? Why? Does he want to tell me about Mavis? Or—I can't be in love with *that man*, can I? He's not at all the gentle understanding man I've always dreamed about. Not at all. He's—almost primitive!

Afterwards, when Jake came into the kitchen to offer help, she fended him off by pointing out that Faith would be a great deal more help in the kitchen, if he would condescend to spend a little time entertaining Mavis. He agreed, but that wide understanding grin of his left Becky even more uncomfortable.

'I'll wash,' Becky told her sister. 'Maybe you could just set the things on the drain for overnight.'

'You know Ma would never let us get away with *that*,' her sister said, picking up the dish-towel. 'Say, he plays pretty rough, don't he? I wonder if he likes kids?'

Becky stopped bustling just long enough to join her at the window. Out by the pool, Jake was giving diving demonstrations off the small board at the deep end of the pool. He was good at it. Mavis was stretched out like a queen on a solitary lounger chair at the far end of the pool, admiring.

'Yes, they make a fine pair,' Becky said. But her tone was at considerable variance with her words. Faith looked up at her and smiled.

'Now, what are you laughing at?' Becky made a full-speed assault on the dishes. She knew from experience that the little secret smile indicated that her sister had just swallowed a comment. 'Well?'

Faith's smile graduated into a giggle. 'You know something?' she started out.

'Why does your generation always have to say "You know"?' Becky interrupted. 'No, I don't know, and obviously you're going to tell me, aren't you?'

'You bet,' Faith returned. 'Dear Becky, did you know you're getting to be a stick-in-the-mud? Ever since you decided to be a doctor you seem to have locked all your funning in a closet somewhere!'

'Ha! Is that so, little miss? Being a doctor is a very time-consuming thing. Doctors have to be dignified. They have to know a lot of things.'

'I'll bet they do,' giggled Faith. 'Like, for example, you've washed that plate three times. Did you know he likes you?'

Becky almost dropped the offending plate on the floor as she turned away to hide her blushes. She didn't realise that the back of her neck turned as red as her cheeks. 'I doubt that very much,' she finally managed to say. 'How in the world do *you* know?'

'How else?' her sister chuckled. 'You can see it. And you like him too! Look at them having such a good time. Is it always that way? Do men have *all* the fun?'

'That's always the way,' Becky returned absentmindedly. She shrugged. 'Poor little female! Learn to run and jump and bow down on command, because that's life, my girl.'

'Come on, now, Becky. You're just trying to change the subject. When did I ever see you or Mama bow down? You *know* you like him!'

'Of course I do,' Becky returned sardonically. 'I like him a lot. Roasted on a big platter with an apple in his mouth!'

They both laughed at each other, straightened out the rest of the kitchen, and went out of the back door hand in hand. 'That Miss Pell, she doesn't seem to do nothing but look decorative,' Faith murmured.

'Yes, there's always that,' chuckled Becky. 'If you're not to be one of the working females, maybe you could be one of the admired ones.'

'Maybe,' Faith returned, looking down at herself in disgust. 'That is, if I can grow into a shape like yours, Becky.'

'Don't worry,' her sister assured her. 'You'll make it. Think about how your mother looks!'

They were still laughing as they came out on to the patio. Jake and Mavis were at the north side of the pool. Becky moved around to the south side and stopped about halfway, where three loungers were placed in a close grouping. Faith flopped into a chair with a sigh of relief, as if she had just completed some tremendous labour.

Almost as soon as they were settled, Jake got up and started to make his way around the pool. Becky stared at him, and blushed when she realised that Mavis was doing the same thing. Two sharks after the same man, Becky thought. And isn't that a strange thought? I'm not really *after* him. If he—if he should just happen, by some chance, to be left lying on the side of the road, with nobody to care about him, I might be—*might* be, mind you—tempted to pick him up and bring him home with me.

He's such a comfortable man to have around, when he's not teasing. Mom was right—it *is* nice to have a man around the house.

Look at those scars, will you? On his back as well as his front, and down his thighs, too. What agony that must have been! There wasn't much that his low-cut trunks concealed. What wasn't on plain view was barely veiled by the cloth. He's a whole lot of man, she told herself. And I'm a whole lot of woman. We'd make a nice pair. At least he wouldn't get a crick in his neck from bending over to kiss me!

That thought was the trigger. She almost felt again

that mass of sensation derived from the last time he had kissed her. The thought made her restless, and she squirmed in her chair, suffering from an itch she could not scratch.

He took the chair closest to her, and his hand crossed the intervening distance and lay over hers. She looked down at it in surprise. Something was going on inside her. And what if I really love him? she asked herself. Lord, I wish Ma were here. I need someone to talk to. The big hand lay over the top of her smaller one, completely encompassing it. There was a warmth, a soothing, comforting warmth.

Left alone on the other side of the pool, Mavis was undecided what to do. There were no empty chairs in that group across the pool, but there was something going on in front of her which she didn't care for in the least. It wasn't like him. This certainly wasn't the wild Jake Meadows she had known for so many years. At this distance, it looked as if he were trying to evade her. Test it out, her conscience commanded. She got up, carefully arranging her patterned skirt, and sauntered around to the other side.

'My, what a cosy little group!' There was a shrill tone in her usually well-controlled voice.

'The triumph of the working class,' Becky offered lazily. It was close on twilight, and shadows hid the little lines of satisfaction that played at the corners of her mouth.

Mavis stood in front of Jake, her weight mostly on one foot, her hand on her hip. It was a practised stance. She had put it to mirror tests by the dozens before adding it to her little repertoire of movements. It projected one lovely hip, and thrust her breasts out as a challenge. He wasn't even looking. She gritted her teeth.

That hand was still bothering Becky—not the weight of it, but rather all it implied. And it was raising havoc in her mind. There had to be something she could do to change the emphasis. She would *not* surrender like some simpering high-school kid!

Mavis was standing there like the Amazon queen, her dress pressed against her as the wind played with it. And here I am with only an old pair of slacks, Becky lectured herself. Even Faith had the sense to get into a nice dress. Damn! The hand, the dress, the well-worn denims she was wearing—that smile on his face. Even in the closing twilight she could see that smile. The hand!

She used both of her very capable hands to pick his up and turn it over. The slight scar from where the fish-hook had caught him was still a line of red against the lighter skin. It was almost hard to see. She raised it up closer to her eyes, 'to examine the surgery,' she told herself. He chuckled and moved closer. A strange madness seized her. The hand kept coming, moving under her direction, but with his power. It came very slowly, palm open, facing upwards. It came to where no seeing was possible. Becky bent her head and kissed the red slash, then cuddled the palm against her cheek.

Mavis spluttered. She said something, but Becky missed it all. She held the hand against her cheek and thrived on the comfort it provided. The other girl said something else, a short expletive, then stormed away into the house. Moments later they saw the lights go on in her bedroom.

'I think I'm getting sleepy,' Faith reported quietly, and sat back in her chair to watch the slow ascent of the moon. After a few minutes of silence she added, 'I think I'll go up myself. The mosquitoes will be coming along any minute now, and we don't want to be eaten alive. Rebecca?'

Becky said not a word. Still holding Jake's warm hand against her cheek, she was lost in a fey dream of love and laughter, babies, home, and all the wonders that lie between man and woman.

CHAPTER SEVEN

A bright sunny day! It peeped in her window, flashed a signal across her eyes, and made Becky welcome when she started and sat up in bed. Oh, what a beautiful morning. It's a singing day, she told herself. There's reason to be happy today, and I don't remember what it is!

She sang herself down to the bathroom, through a tepid shower, and into her best slacks and silk shirt. Shoes in hand, she padded down the stairs and into the kitchen. Mavis Pell was already there, sitting at the kitchen table.

'Good morning,' Becky sang as she walked over to open the curtains. 'Look at that! Not a cloud in the sky!'

'Is that supposed to mean something?' The other woman sounded as if mice had slept in her mouth. 'It was just as sunny yesterday. And the day before, come to think of it.'

'Well—perhaps it was.' Becky balanced on tiptoe for the coffee pot, and was in too sweet a mood for argument. How about another angle? 'You're up early, aren't you?'

'You're darn well right,' Mavis returned bitterly. 'Can we have some of that coffee in a hurry?'

'Not perked,' Becky reported. 'That takes twenty minutes. I could whip up some instant coffee in a jiffy?'

'Yes; lord, yes. Anything, so long as it's quick and hot.'

And so that seems to end *that* conversation, Becky told herself. Her hands sped to their tasks, uncontrolled. Her mind was filled with other thoughts. Why is Mavis up at dawn? Did she and Jake have another fight? They *did* meet again last night. At least, I know she stole out of the house and went down to his cabin at some time close to

100

midnight. Are they—or am I just a fool, daydreaming? One kiss, one kind word, one evening of holding hands, and what do I make out of it. Orange blossoms and wedding dresses, of course, just like any kid fresh out of school. Is *he* for real?

Speculating was not a help. There was something different about her guest. What the devil was it? Dressed, of course. She was dressed in shorts and a tank top, instead of one of her more usual exquisite dresses. They *did* meet after the rest of us had gone to bed.

'Going out today?' Becky hazarded. Mavis wrapped both hands around her coffee mug, as if to draw down its heat. She looked up with a mixed expression on her face.

'Yeah,' she muttered. 'We're going blueberrying. Can you imagine that? Mavis Pell gets up early in the morning to go blueberry picking. That ought to rate a few lines in the Albany papers!'

Becky's hands kept working. She was getting better at the game. It almost seemed possible to keep the pain shut up in her heart. They *did* meet. And spend the night? At least they made up their little spat, you fool! Becky Latimore, prize fool of all New England. A little kiss, some hand-holding, and—presto—he's back in the good graces of the society queen! As Becky moved around the kitchen, her long black hair swinging loosely to every change, the other woman followed her with her eyes.

The question came out of the clear blue sky. 'Do you love him?'

Becky stopped with her frying pan in mid-air. 'Him who?'

'You know. Jake.'

Becky swallowed. What was there to say? 'Love him? Where would you get that idea? I can hardly stand the man! And I don't understand how his books sell. I would think an author must reflect himself in his writing.'

'Oh, his books sell all right.' Mavis chuckled as she

took another sip of coffee. 'But to a restricted clientele, you know.'

'I knew it,' Becky snapped as she stuffed the toaster. 'Pornography, you mean!'

'That's the best description I've heard yet,' giggled Mavis. 'Pornography! Well, there are a lot of naked bodies lying around. I tried to read one once, but I barely made it to page ten. But those who *can* suffer through them think he's wonderful!'

'So does he,' Becky muttered.

'Say, you really don't like him, do you!' The idea seemed to pick up her guest's spirits immensely. 'I thought—last night—well, he was making a play for you, and I figured that all the hand-holding——'

She stopped in mid-sentence as Becky mustered a half-hysterical laugh. 'His hand,' she gulped. 'I did some minor surgery on his hand, and hadn't seen it for a few days.'

'Oh! I keep forgetting that you're a doctor. You don't look old enough for that.'

'Thank you—I think.' Becky took a long hard look at the other woman. Those harsh lines around her mouth were fading, and there was a small sparkle in her eyes. Why, if it weren't for the circumstances, Becky thought, I might even end up liking this lady. She was about to make some inane comment along those lines when the kitchen door banged open and Faith rushed in.

'Are you going to fix breakfast?' The girl rubbed at still-sleepy eyes, and moved to her appointed place at the kitchen table. 'Becky?'

'Oh, my,' Becky responded. 'I was daydreaming. What was it you wanted for breakfast?'

'Pancakes, with maple syrup, please?'

'I'm not sure we have all the ingredients,' her sister responded. She went back to the side table and weighed the box of flour in her hand. The pies had taken a considerable portion from their stores, and there was

barely enough left for pancakes. She stretched for the
ingredients, but even being a tall girl didn't seem to help.
Everything was on the top shelf. Which only showed, she
told herself, that you should never let a man do the
unpacking. She tried a little jump, and missed. Shrugging
her shoulders, she made ready to jump again.

A pair of large hands seized her around the waist and
carefully put her to one side. 'What——' she spluttered.
Jake Meadows, of course, who else could it be.

'The flour box and the syrup bottle,' he said over his
shoulder as he nonchalantly brought the materials down
on to the table. Becky wiped her hands nervously on her
apron.

'I hadn't expected to see you this morning,' she stated
flatly. She took the pancake flour from him and moved
over to the stove.

'Lovely day,' he commented to all and sundry.

'Is it?' asked Mavis as she rested both elbows on the
table and cupped her chin with both hands.

'Nice,' Faith contributed. She was already up to her
elbows in a heavily buttered piece of toast while waiting
for the main course.

'That's not bad,' Jake commented. 'Two out of three.
Not half bad. Are you ready for the expedition, Mavis?'

'As ready as I'm ever going to be,' she returned.
'Blueberries. What the devil would we do with a bucket
of blueberries? Provided, of course, that there are some
out there.'

'Oh, they're out there, all right. The marshland at the
south end of the lake is full of them.'

'And there are always heaps of them by Elder Creek,'
Becky offered.

'So we'll get a dozen baskets of berries, and then
what?' Mavis was worrying that bone to death, trying to
jolt Jake out of his plans for the day, without much luck.

'I suppose I could always make each of you a pie,'
Becky suggested. 'But—well, I have to go into town

anyway. We're almost out of any kind of flour, and other things.'

'So there,' Jake chuckled. 'All your fancies have been blown away, Mavis. Ready to start? Faith, would you like to go with us?'

A frown flashed across the child's face. She looked over at her sister, an appeal on her face that said, as plainly as any words could, that she didn't want to go.

'Becky?'

'I don't think Faith should——'

'And suppose I wanted to take you?' She backed away from him.

'Not me,' she protested. 'I've got enough to do. Including going into Stockbridge to buy flour.'

'Chicken,' he taunted, 'It would be a wonderful day— all that sun, lovely company. Can Faith come?'

'Oh, no. I have to take her with me. It's a long drive, you know. And besides, Ma says it's time to start training her.'

'Witchcraft lessons?'

'Housekeeping lessons. You think girls are born with that in their genes? And it is a terrible drive.'

'So we know, lady,' he laughed. 'We made it by moonlight.'

'And I thought I was going to be killed,' grumbled Mavis. 'Have you ever seen this fool drive by moonlight?'

'I can't say I've seen him drive in any condition,' Becky muttered under her breath. 'But that's it? You two go berrying, and Faith goes with me?'

'Yes,' answered Jake. Mavis pouted. She's not really an outdoor girl, Becky sighed to herself. Too bad!

Faith walked with Becky down to the dock to see the water-borne expedition start. Mavis was already being inducted into the art of boating. Jake had handed her the bailing can, and her face reflected her disgust as she made a few ineffectual swipes at the bilge water.

It was still a beautiful day, with not a cloud in the sky. A dive-bombing pair of bluebirds followed the jeep along the narrow track that called itself a road. Becky stopped for a moment at the curve where Darcy Creek poured into the main run of the Tiquonet River. A family of beavers were hard at work trying to dam the creek, but hard work had not yet overcome high water.

'They'll never get it dammed,' laughed Faith. 'All that work wasted!'

'Don't you believe it,' Becky returned. 'They'll keep trying—and trying. And on one of those tries they'll make that link to the other shoreline—and that will be the triumph of need over Nature. You just watch. I wouldn't be surprised to see it done by the time we come back. Bet?'

'Aw, Becky, like Ma says, you're always the optimist. If you keep on this way you'll be the poorest doctor in New England.'

'Maybe,' her sister laughed. 'But are you going to put your money where your mouth is?'

'Well——!'

'Bet?'

'Okay now, let me get this straight. You're betting me that the beavers will have finished a dam across this creek by the time we get back?'

'Oh, no, you don't, wise guy! I'm betting you a buck that the beavers will have established a first link across the creek by the time we come back. One dollar says it's so!'

'Well——'

'What's the matter? Cold feet?'

'Nope. It's just that a buck is awful small. How about two?'

'All right, two!' Becky shifted gear and started off down the trail again. 'Boy, Pop's right!' she yelled as the dam site disappeared around the bend. 'He keeps saying you ought to be a lawyer.'

'Well, I will.' Faith shifted in her seat and looked over at her sister earnestly. 'You and Mattie got all the brains and beauty—so I asked Pop what else the company needed.'

'And he said?' Becky coaxed.

'And he said that, after the way Mama took them all to the cleaners, what the company needed was a good lawyer he could be sure would be on *his* side. So that's what I'm gonna do!' Since the story had been told more than once around the fireplace, how their mother had whipped the Latimore Corporation to a standstill in a four-year law case, the joke needed no further explanation.

The bumpy ride discouraged conversation. When they reached Killdevil Gorge, the place where the Tiquonet River plunged through the only gap in the Berkshires before drifting downhill into New York State, Becky pulled over into a brace of pines, a puzzled look on her face.

'What's the matter?' Faith unstrapped her seatbelt and climbed out to stretch her legs. It had been a battering, mauling drive from the beaver dam to this narrow gorge. The river took up most of the gap between the cliffs. The remaining space contained the one-track dirt road.

'Look at the road,' Becky said quietly.

'Look at the road? Why—it's narrower, isn't it? Is the river coming up or something?'

'Don't be silly, love. There hasn't been a drop of rain in these parts in almost three months. We're in the middle of a major drought. No, I don't think the river's coming up. I think the road is slipping off the rock shelf! Come over here, carefully.' The two of them moved to the edge of the road, where the river current swept along at a powerful pace. 'Now, hold my hand, Faith, and for God's sake don't let go!'

The younger girl dug both heels in, extended a hand,

and watched while her older sister stepped gently forward almost to the water's edge. One slight inch further she moved, and the gravel beneath her feet began to slip and slide into the river.

'That does it!' gasped Becky, pulling herself back. 'Come on. We need the supplies, and we can't waste any time!' When they had both buckled up she edged the vehicle so close against the cliff that the bumpers scraped against the rock, then pushed the gas pedal down until the jeep jumped forwards. They were quickly clear of the danger, out into the open segment of Lebanon Valley. The echoes of the pulsing engine still filled the air as they stopped on the other side.

'Becky,' Faith gasped, 'look—up there!' They both shaded their eyes and glanced up the face of the cliff. Some hundred feet above them a particularly sharp knob was vibrating in synchronisation with the engine noises. As they watched, the cliff itself splattered a few rocks and some fine dust down on to the trail. 'Right,' Becky announced. 'We need the food, but we won't go into town. There's that little general store on Route 183.'

It was almost eleven when the tired crew of berry pickers rowed slowly towards the dock. That their trip had proved successful was amply demonstrated by the filled pails in the bottom of the boat. But the pickers didn't look too happy. The picker, perhaps that should be. A grumpy Mavis Pell sat on the middle seat, mud-covered, glaring at the world. Behind her, back to them all, Jake heaved gently on the oars to bring them up to the dock.

'Can't you hurry?' Mavis hissed at him for the tenth time.

'Nope,' he returned. 'My doctor's watching. She's got a mean temper when it comes to rowing boats.'

'I didn't come all this way to listen to some hick doctor,' snapped Mavis. He hushed her with a finger. 'Take a look,' he said. 'The others have got back, and there's something wrong. Get that line ready, and let's see if we can moor this ark.'

There seemed to be a conspiracy of silence on the dock. Faith came down to the boat and took the mooring line from Mavis. When Jake stepped out on to the dock Faith motioned him silently to the jeep, which was parked as close to the dock as the road would allow. He started to say something, but Faith shook her head. His long strides quickly took him to where Becky was waiting, at the back of the jeep.

The two down at the boat could see them exchange a few words, the blonde head and the raven curls bent over a map.

'What . . .?' Mavis started to ask. Faith shushed her, and beckoned her out of the boat. The stern line was made fast. Feeling the tension, they all hurried up the dock to the jeep.

'I can't help how many hundred years it's been there,' Becky was stating very firmly. 'So maybe Hiawatha stood up there and smoked a peace pipe. That was then. This is now. The whole face of the cliff is coming down— hell, not coming down—came down. We were past it, about a quarter of a mile down the road, and we *saw* it come down!'

'You actually saw it fall?'

'I actually saw it fall. Dust and dirt and rocks all over the place, and there's a blockage on the road that's maybe—oh—sixty feet up in the air. And half the river is dammed, too. The water was cutting around behind us when we took off down the road!'

'Well.' Jake was speaking slowly, evidently trying to rally his troops. 'So it means we might be cut off for a day or two,' he reported. 'After all, they sent a helicopter in to pick up your mother, didn't they?'

'Yes,' Becky said morosely. 'And that's the chopper they sent down to New Jersey to monitor the contract extension of the Garden State Parkway.'

'It can't be the only helicopter in Massachusetts,' Mavis snapped. 'I want out of here today!'

'Well, good luck to you,' retorted Faith.

'Hey, I don't understand the problem,' Jake contributed. 'We're all happy here, so what the devil do we need a chopper for?'

'I'll tell you if you don't know,' said Mavis forcefully, 'If you think this was my idea of a fine day, let me convince you otherwise.'

The argument rose to a crescendo. Becky and Faith exchanged glances and wandered down the pier to keep out of range of projectiles. But the verbal war followed them, as the other couple came along behind them. There was no escape. The two Latimore women stood their ground at the very edge of the dock.

'And it's all your fault!' Mavis screeched at Becky. 'You and that stupid sister of yours!' Becky's head jerked up. Nothing disturbed her more than criticism of her family.

'Leave my sister out of this,' she snapped. 'If you want to fight, pick on someone your own size!'

'That does it!' snarled Mavis. 'Where's that damned radio? I'm going to call a helicopter and get out of this rats' nest!'

'Go ahead,' Becky returned. 'But don't expect us to help. You know, Mavis, deep down inside you're a rotten person!'

The shriek that went up was about as wild as anything Becky had ever heard. The next action caught her completely off guard. The wild-eyed blonde, frustrated beyond her breaking point, put both hands in the middle of Becky's back and pushed.

She hit the water in a terrific belly-whopper that knocked the breath out of her. But once over the initial shock, Becky's humour took over. After all, it had been a long six-hour drive over dusty trails, and she needed a bath. The lake was warm, her clothes would not suffer from immersion, and—it had to be admitted—Mavis had some right to complain: the Latimores had hardly treated her as a treasured guest during the last few days!

And so, while the three of them on the dock peered down at her, Becky rolled over on her back and stroked herself out a few feet and ducked underwater. And, being underwater, she missed the second shriek. Becky came up just in time to see Mavis Pell execute a rudimentary swan dive, and sister Faith rub her hands together in a satisfied manner. Jake was standing there with his hands in his pockets, seemingly very interested in a pair of birds flying in off the lake.

Becky hardly cared to continue the encounter, so she turned over, went into her best Australian crawl, and was at the dock's access ladder in a moment. As she climbed up she could hear Mavis screaming behind her.

'I can't swim!' she was shouting. 'I can't swim!'

'So why don't you try standing up?' Faith called down to her. 'The water's only three feet deep out there!'

There was a cessation of splashing, a few unladylike words muttered carefully, and Mavis's head appeared above the ladder as she climbed huffily back on to the wharf. Stirred out of his lethargy, Jake went over to lend a hand.

'You little—monster!' She could have won a first prize at any hog-calling contest. All the civilised veneer was stripped away. 'That little monster pushed me!'

'As you pushed me,' snapped Becky. 'Here's your handbag, lady.'

Mavis snatched it up without a word of thanks or excuse, and stormed at Meadows.

'I want out of here—right now! You get me out of here!' Her voice was rising into the hysterical range. Becky, bothered at last by conscience, snatched a blanket from the jeep, wrapped it around the woman, and tugged her up towards the beach. The soaked woman dug in her heels. 'Not with you!' she shouted. 'Not with any of you—you murderers!'

Becky shrugged her shoulders at Jake and gestured up the trail. He took charge, wrapping the blanket more tightly around Mavis's shoulders, then picked her up and threw her over his shoulder and started for the house on top of the hill.

Becky had the doors open before they arrived, and the radio turned on. 'I want a helicopter right now!' Mavis screamed.

'We have to wait until the radio warms up,' Becky said quietly. Her answer brought her a long line of gibberish and insults, but she shrugged them off. Her training told her just how close the woman was to complete hysteria. The radio began to make rushing sounds, then settled down to the intermittent bell tone that Latimore Corporation used to mark its communication channel. Becky took one big swallow and pushed the 'talk' switch.

'Latimore Control, this is Latimore.' Silence. She repeated the call. A rusty voice, filtering through static crashes, came back to her. 'This is Latimore Control. Who is calling, please?'

She was so eager to get the job done that she fumbled her fingers off the switch and dropped the microphone on the floor. She was on it like a hawk, squeezing the switch before she regained her feet. 'Latimore Control,' she shouted, 'this is Becky—Becky Latimore!'

'Becky Latimore?' the clear cool voice enquired. 'Your father's not here.' There was a pause, and then the voice again, not cool at all, 'But our Mr Riley wants to speak to you.'

Becky took a deep breath and collapsed in the chair by the instrument. 'But our Mr Riley . . .' Her second father. The man who took care of all her troubles when Pop was away—and had, ever since the two of them had stood on the steps of the Hall in Eastboro, and watched Mama and Pop drive away on their honeymoon.

'Becky?' The voice was husky, gravelly with age. 'Where are you, girl?'

'I—we're all up here at Lake Mohawk, Uncle Charlie.'

'At Lake Mohawk? There's been some tremendous foul-up. Damn computer! It isn't worth . . . Becky,' and then off the microphone to someone else close to him, 'where the hell is that map!' Silence, for a moment, and then, 'Becky girl, how many of you are there out there?'

'Faith and myself,' she answered, 'and two other people. Uncle Charlie, we——'

'Becky! You've got a vehicle, I suppose? Get yourself out of there, all of you, as fast as you can move!'

'But we can't, Uncle Charlie', she half-cried into the microphone. 'We can't get out by road—there's been a big cave-in at Killdevil Gorge, and the road is closed to all traffic. Couldn't you send a chopper?'

There was another moment of silence, broken only by sporadic radio noises. 'Did you say you can't get out by road? Over.'

'That's a Roger. We can't get out by road. There's been a tremendous cave-in at the gorge. We couldn't even climb over it. Is there some trouble with sending a chopper?'

The silence was deafening. 'Uncle Charlie?'

The microphone at the other end was switched on again. 'How many of you are there?'

'Three adults and——' Becky stopped. Unflappable Faith was kicking at her ankle, her face flushed. 'Correction,' Becky said quickly. 'We have four adults here. What's the matter, Uncle Charlie?' She could feel the tiniest shiver run up and down her spine. Everything was *sure* to be okay. Three men she trusted with all her life and love: Pop, her big brother Henry, and Uncle Charlie. And yet she had this feeling—this terrible feeling.

The voice came back to her again, clear and full of pain. 'The problem is, my darling, that there's a terrible forest fire raging to the west of you and moving in your direction. There's so much smoke and flame that it's almost impossible to manoeuvre a chopper in the area. We've placed most of our aircraft at the disposal of the Governor's emergency committee. That leaves us with just the one old Sikorsky, and, besides the pilot, all that it could lift out would be one adult.'

Becky, holding her breath, looked around the group. All of their faces showed the strain—except Jake's. She could almost see him shrug his shoulders as if it were not too terribly important. He nodded to her, the slightest movement of his head, which contained a whole message. A massive gust of wind struck at the house. She pushed down the button on the microphone.

'Uncle Charlie? Send it, please. The storm is coming at us now. We'll shove in as many as it can hold, and the rest will just have to take care of themselves.'

'Roger, Becky—as soon as we can. Watch out. According to our last reports the fire is coming straight up the valley at high speed. It's gale winds and a crown fire!'

Becky set the microphone down on the desk and started to breathe again. Her rib-cage ached from the strain. Another smashing blow from the wind bounced the house.

Mavis was standing at Faith's side, her face pallid. The child stood straight-backed, composed. She knew, she understood, and her Latimore courage was holding firm.

And him. *That man*. Becky felt a curious detachment. To have found a man like him, and lose him, all in one mad storm. What a shame. What nice children we could have had! Her eyes traced his face, making an imprint in her heart, and a shiver ran up her back. 'Somebody's walking over my grave,' she muttered, and put it all out of mind.

Mavis was the one to worry about. Her face was stark

white, and her lips moved back and forth with no sounds coming out. One little lady about to go over the edge completely, Becky's training told her. She registered the fact, but no treatment suggested itself. So she'll go into hysterics. And promptly scare Faith half to death, if not further. Jake was watching like a hawk, but doing nothing.

Becky's neat and compartmented mind ran down the list of drugs available in her little black bag. Valium, of course. One or two neat quick jabs would leave the lovely Miss Pell a walking zombie, with everything coming up roses. Except she couldn't remember where she had left her black bag. In the jeep? Upstairs? Down at the dock? Her mind returned no answer, and Mavis's lips were moving back and forth faster and faster. Two more seconds—three at the most and the fat would be in the fire! What to do? She looked squarely at Jake; he was laughing at her. Oh, well, she told herself; I've always wanted to try this sort of anaesthetic, anyway.

She balled up the fingers of her right hand, tested them against the open palm of her left, and just as Mavis opened her mouth to scream, Becky swung her right hand in a long loping curve, just over the woman's shoulder, and firmly on her quivering chin. The scream turned into a squeak. Mavis collapsed ever so gently into Jake Meadows' arms, and he wrapped her up in another blanket.

'Nice work, Doctor,' he murmured. Nobody else seemed to have noticed.

I must find that bag of mine, Becky told herself sternly. Her knuckles were sore and the skin had split open on two of them. He raised her hand to his mouth and gently nursed the cuts. No wonder boxers make so much money! she told herself, as his tongue played havoc with her nerves.

CHAPTER EIGHT

THE radio that served the little house deep in the Berkshires was but a tiny segment of a much larger system. From the living-room of the house at Lake Mohawk it bounced its message to an unattended radio repeater sitting inside a stone building on top of Mount Becker, then relayed itself to another building on top of Mount Greylock, from which it was hurled across the rest of the state to an antenna on top of the John Hancock Building. Through a dozen cables it climbed down the building, and out into a large computer-crammed room that was the control room of the Latimore Corporation. Two young women were constantly on duty, switching signals around to various offices of the Corporation. When Becky's conversation with Charlie Riley was concluded, a red light appeared on the huge wall-map that filled one side of the room. It wandered around for a second, then settled down as near as the map would show on Lake Mohawk. It froze in position there, and a little bell rang four times. The half-dozen men in the room looked up all at the same time.

'What the hell!' one of the younger men complained. 'We don't have any work up there in the mountains. What's going on?' One of the two women at the signals desk had already started to answer his question. The red light was now circled by a green one. Experienced fingers chased down code lists and found Green—Major Forest Fire. And then the red light started to blink. There was no need to consult code lists. Blinking red—Company personnel in Danger.

A slide projector facing the wall adjacent to the map lit up, its white light bright against the dim lighting of the room. An electronic typewriter began to project a list of names: 'Company personnel, Rebecca Latimore, Faith Latimore; others: Mavis Pell, unknown; Jake Meadows, unknown.' The typewriter went silent. The names hung there, gleaming against the darkness.

'Good God!' somebody in the background swore. 'Where the hell are those trucks? Northampton? There's a bulldozer in Lenox.' The computer keyboard was punched again. A few more words appeared on the screen. 'No land escape passage. Killdevil Gorge closed by landslide.'

'Where's the boss?' The question was hushed. The computer keyboard clicked again. 'Bermuda,' the screen flashed. 'Executive jet now refuelling on standby at that station.' The computer clicked one more time, and messages went out to strange destinations as the machine contacted other machines and transferred information. Over in the dark corner, back turned to them all, a grey-haired man held a microphone in his hand and fired off a large number of words prohibited by law.

'I don't give a damn that you just landed, Elmer! You get that whirlybird of yours in the air right now. I'll tell you where to go when you get up. Don't argue with me, man, or you'll need a new bushing for your rear end! I told you who was there. Are you in the air yet? Only fifty feet? My God, I got buzzards can fly faster than that! Head west. Lake Mohawk. There's a forest fire, and two of the boss's kids are caught in it. Wouldn't you know it would be Becky. How many? There's three adults and one kid. Yes, I *know* you can't take them all out, but you gotta do the best you can. Are you up to a thousand feet yet? Elmer, if that orange crate of yours don't get going I'm gonna put one arm down your throat and pull your heart out—if you've got one. Yes. I said Becky!'

'Why is she so important? Because she's the oldest, and she's adopted, and she's my special girl-friend. You think you'll have trouble with the boss if Becky don't come out right? You just sit back and think what'll happen if her mother, Mary Kate, hears about it. Get moving, you superannuated idiot!'

And of all the signals and summaries and computer print-outs, that one conversation did the most good.

The tiny voice over the radio chimed in again, and silenced every other noise in the room. There was just the tiniest tremble in it. 'Uncle Charlie? Is he coming, Uncle Charlie?'

The old man grabbed the microphone back from the secretary. 'He's coming, love. He's at a thousand feet now, just over South Hadley, someplace. He says he can see the smoke. Now you just worry about how you're going to cram all those people into one little Sikorsky.'

The voice was weaker, breaking up. 'I—I don't know, Uncle Charlie. The smoke is everywhere now. The fire's jumping along the tops of the trees. I can't see the lake from here. I think we'll lose the generator building pretty quickly. I——' There was a crashing noise, and a couple of side statements. 'Don't worry about it,' a deep male voice said. 'I'll take care of her. Tell your pilot to come down in the middle of the lake and then move towards shore. The flames are almost at the roof of the house now. We'll have to pull out before they cut us off from the lake. Now, mind this. We'll get as many as we can on that chopper, and the rest of us will shelter in the lake. This has to be our last transmission. And if you're worried about it, call the headquarters of the Massachusetts National Guard and tell them that Jake Meadows is out here.'

The microphone cut off with a deadly snap. The Operations Room went quiet. Charlie Riley strolled over to one of the windows, stared out, and saw nothing. He had been working for the Latimore Corporation for fifteen years or more when Bruce Latimore had set out to prove Mary Kate was a country cousin. And Charlie had been the best man at their wedding. He remembered it all, and there was a tear squeezing under his eyelid. When the secretary waved the telephone at him he walked over and took it.

'Brigadier General Wilson,' she said. He shrugged his shoulders. To people from the giant Latimore Corporation, one-star generals were a dime a dozen.

'Who's Jake Meadows?' he barked into the instrument. And then listened. And listened. And listened. When he put the telephone down he did it carefully, as if he were afraid it might break. Everyone in the Operations Room was staring at him. He clasped his hands behind his back, harrumphed to clear his throat, and went back to the windows. 'They'll be all right,' he commented over his shoulder. The atmosphere behind him brightened. Breathing could be heard, and conversation.

Jake set the microphone down gently on the table and switched off the transceiver. Becky stood stiffly next to him, her hands along the seams of her slacks, biting at her lip. 'It's not me,' she said in a strained voice. 'It's Faith. Mom and Pop don't deserve that kind of pain and worry. They're used to it with me, but not with Faith. I wish——'

'Listen,' he said softly, pulling her hard up against him and tipping her chin back. 'There's no place *you* can call for assurance that Jake Meadows will get you out. You just have to trust me. I *will* get you out. Trust me?'

It was hard for her to swallow. All her ambivalent feelings about him had evaporated. She was overwhelmed with the loving of him. There was a spark in his eye—she hadn't seen that before. He looked more and more like an adventuring buccaneer—and he had given her a promise.

'Yes,' she said very softly. 'What do you want me to do?'

'First of all, the child. How can we best handle her?'

'Give Faith something to do—something to be responsible for, and she'll hang on all right. It's Mavis. I can't knock her out again. She needs a sedative, or she's going to blow up in the world. I don't remember where I left my bag.'

'Okay. And what does Becky Latimore need?'

'Lord, I don't know. They were laying artillery fire down on our hospital when I was in Chad—three, four times a day. It didn't bother me too much. And then a mosquito bit me and I fell apart. I'm not a very good chief, but I can make a pretty fair Indian.'

'Well, how about if I prescribe for you, Doctor Latimore? What you need in the next twelve hours is a lot of faith and love.'

'And who'll administer that?'

'Me, girl.' He leaned over just far enough to touch his lips to hers, and then broke the contact. It was the warmth that did it; the casual touch of warmth. He took her by the shoulders, turned her around, and patted her gently on her bottom. 'Your little black bag is out in the kitchen on the floor,' he told her. 'Go give Miss Pell enough of something for a long night's sleep.'

It was almost like being in the emergency room in the hospital where she had done her first training. She smiled at him and walked out into the kitchen. Faith was following Becky with her eyes; she paced herself until she heard Jake talking to the girl.

'Faith!' he called. 'Over here.' The child moved on command. 'Fires are a big problem to some people,' he said in a man-to-woman tone. 'Your sister has had a great deal to cope with in the past few hours, and now it's up to you and me to keep things under control, right?'

The little girl looked up at him hesitantly. 'I—I ain't too brave about fires myself,' she stammered.

'But we have a responsibility, you and I,' he said solemnly. 'Becky has been taking care of all of us, and now it's time for us to take care of her. Don't you think so?'

'I—well—yes.' Responsibility was the key word, Jake mused. All these Latimore women responded to it, like a fireman to an alarm bell. Faith's determination was being screwed up to meet the challenge. He could see the wheels turning in her little head.

'Okay. Now—we're going down to the lake in just a minute. You go over and get Becky by the hand and hang on until Hell won't have it. You understand?'

'Yup. My brother Henry says that all the time.'

'And you're not scared?'

'I'm scared. But I'll do it—honest I will.'

'Good. Now, when we start I'm going to be carrying Miss Pell over my shoulder, and I'm going to follow Becky and yourself. This is my shirt-tail, right? As soon as we start to move, you grab Becky with one hand as hard as you can, and hang on to my shirt-tail with the other. Got it?'

'Like in the movies?' A tiny smile flickered on her pale face.

'Only maybe a little hotter. Ready?'

'Yessir.'

Becky came back at that moment. Yessir? Faith only said that to her father, and then only as a last resort—as, for example, when talking back to him.

She smiled at the thought as she moved over to the couch where Mavis Pell was still stretched out. Good job, Becky congratulated herself. That's the first person I've hit in anger since I was sixteen. Harry Fenton, that had been. He had suddenly developed a pair of octopus hands. And now then, Miss Pell, I'm about to fix your little red wagon. A swab of alcohol, a careful shaking of the container, a quick injection. She wiped the puncture site again with the alcohol swab, and looked for a place to throw it. Oh, God, she told herself, the whole world is burning down and I'm looking for a sanitary disposal unit!

'She's ready,' she called over to Jake as she fastened a tag around Mavis's wrist stating the date, size, and identification of the injection. He came at once, waited while she repacked her bag, then slung Miss Pell over his right shoulder in a fireman's lift.

'You first,' he commanded softly. 'Stop long enough at my cabin to get some rope. Keep your eyes on the tops of the trees, and keep low. If the smoke comes in on us, try to keep underneath it, even if you have to crawl. But whatever you do, don't stop moving. If the scrub pine at the shore is burning, go into the water as far as you can— without walking your sister underwater. Got it?'

'Yes.' And then, because that sounded too curt, 'Yes, sir.'

He laughed and gestured her towards the front door. As soon as he started to move, Faith was there hanging on to his shirt-tail, and clutching Becky with her other hand. The procession went out like an elephant parade, nose to tail.

It hardly seemed a big problem to Becky when first they started off. But the first step off the front porch snatched her breath away. The fire was running in the tops of the trees, and the heat created a wild uprush of air to feed it, sweeping everything loose upwards, in a wild witch-dance, until it, too, fell into the flames, blossomed quickly, and was gone. Becky hesitated for just that little half-step, looked back at Jake over her shoulder, dipped into his quiet courage and started down the path. His one free hand caught up with her and clutched at her own slender hand, confirming the bond between them. 'Oh, God,' she whispered, 'keep us together to a happier time!'

It became more difficult to breathe. Not only was the air hot, but also there didn't seem to be much of it, even though the smoke trail was well above their heads. Becky

stifled a tiny whimper, bent over further, and plunged
down the hill.

There was no need to bend and twist around the tufts
and bushes that had formerly defined the path. They
were all gone. But the footwork needed to avoid the
charred embers was considerable. Warily, holding
hard against terror, she led them downwards.

When the lake came in sight she stumbled to a stop. A
pall of smoke covered the entire area, hanging about fifty
feet above the water. A rim of fire ran riot among the
trees atop the surrounding cliffs. Her courage dropped
another two inches. There was just no way that a
helicopter could find its way in through the maze of fire
and smoke.

Faith must have felt her fear. A jerk at her hand and an
extra squeeze brought her to the problem behind her. She
flashed the child a trembling smile over her shoulder.
The girl's face was pale, concentrating as only a child
can, but with not a sign of fear. In fact, she looked as if
she were taking a stroll in some garden. Becky's heart
swelled. Even in this terrible time, she told herself, I'm
proud to be a Latimore.

Jake tugged them to a halt before they went past his
cabin. Built low as it was, it sat serenely amid the
carnage. He dropped Mavis to the ground and dashed
into the cabin. As he went, Becky leaned back and stole a
look at the house above them. For one gracious moment
it was there, wreathed in smoke, an anchor to memory.
And then it exploded in flames, like the burst of a
skyrocket, flinging embers all over the area.

Faith was watching at the same time. Her jaw fell open
and she moved closer to her sister. Becky smiled down at
her as if this were something to be expected. Faith was
convinced. 'Pretty,' she said nonchalantly, and dismissed
the entire incident from her mind.

Jake Meadows was back with a coil of rope over his
shoulder. He swept up the unconscious woman, reached

for Becky's hand, and yelled 'shirt-tail' at Faith. The parade resumed.

It was more difficult now. The flames were dropping below the crowns of the trees, and down their creosote-laden trunks. The level of smoke came down with them. Bent almost double, Becky screwed up her courage and led the way. They were more than two-thirds of the way to the water. She kept telling herself that as she fumbled forward. Once she stopped and jumped to one side as a flaming branch crashed down on to the path. Only the pressure of his hand on hers kept her under control. She could hear Faith, now, whimpering.

It was a surprise to her to realise that below the smoke level there actually seemed to be more oxygen. The fires were still burning, but the temperature was dropping. Not fast, not greatly, but enough to allow them to treasure a breath or two. As the parade leader, Becky stepped up her speed. The path from this point downwards was wider, too. More sand, less loose debris, fewer tall trees around from which burning brands might plummet.

She was talking to herself as she half-ran, panting. 'Only a few more steps. Only a few more steps. Only a few more——' She stopped the conversation and began to giggle. Her feet were in water—safe, blessed water. She stifled her hysteria, whirled around past him, and snatched Faith up in her arms.

'We've done it, darling!' she shouted at her.

Joy, great relief, has to have an outlet, a moment of release. Jake was standing a few feet away. He had dropped the coil of rope at the edge of the sandy beach and was stretching Mavis Pell out, with her body in the water and her head on the sand. He stood up as if it were an effort, and before she could give it all a second thought, or he a first, she jumped at him, throwing her arms around his neck as his arms automatically swept around to hold her loosely in front of him.

It wasn't looseness she wanted. In all the madness of the fire, all the fear, all the faltering, a new emotion had been forged in her soul, tempered by fire. Her arms tightened around his neck with all her strength, almost a stranglehold, while her feet squirmed as she struggled to get closer to him, to become a part of him.

He hesitated, and then responded. His arms gathered her in protectively, one hand under her thighs, the other behind her back, bringing her head up on to his chest just under his chin. There was strength there, and something more. He gently squeezed her rib-cage and smiled down at her without speaking. Gently, slowly, his big hand moved up over her ample breast and squeezed again.

She wanted more than that. She wanted the pain of success. She swept one hand out from around his neck, dropped it on top of his own, and squeezed with all her strength.

There was no telling were it might have led, this erotic impulse of hers, because that was the moment when Faith's courage broke down. She squatted down in the water and began to cry. Becky knew it was the final appeal; the little girl was calling for her mother. Becky pecked a kiss at Jake's lips, and he let her slide gently down on to her own feet. Then he crouched down to comfort Faith. It was a time for comforting. The mad clouds of smoke, whipped by the wind, were dropping lower and lower. They could see no more than two hundred feet in any direction, and the flaming trees wore fire blossoms, whipped by the wind.

Jake sat down in the water, pulled Faith against him to get her completely wet—and then stiffened. They both heard the motor. Luckily for their mental health, they could not hear the radio report that the helicopter was throwing out into the relay system.

'What can you see?' the Operations Room operator asked.

'Not a damn thing,' Elmer reported, 'Is Charlie still there?'

'Yes, what is it?' growled Riley. 'Where the hell are you?'

'I'm on top of a big pile of chocolate pudding,' the pilot reported. 'It stretches—oh, ten miles by five. I can't see the lake or the cliffs. The wind is murder down there.'

'You can't see anything in it?'

'I told you. What the hell do you think I am—a magician?'

'So what are you going to do?'

'I'm gonna do two things, Charlie Riley. First, I wanna remind you we've worked together for thirty years now, and you're as much of a son of a bitch now as you was in the beginning. And second. I'm gonna find the centre of this damn pudding, and I'm gonna go down until I hit something, or it hits me. You wanna say somethin' else?'

'Hell, no, Elmer. I admit it all. Take a deep breath before you go in. And God be with you. You're one hell of a pilot!'

The helicopter jockeyed for position over the rising windy screen of smoke, until Elmer thought he might at least be over water, and then he started the descent slowly, inches at a time. Willingly, gently, he went into the darkness. It was more difficult to keep the craft on an even keel, now that his speed was reduced. He sucked gently at the tube of the oxygen mask that was standard on all air-rescue missions. The smoke was infiltrating the cockpit. covering his instruments. But after forty years of flying, he didn't need them anyway. He could still fly by the seat of his pants!

It was that last thought that almost scuppered him. Pride coming before a fall. In one instant he was flying in a cloud of smoke; in the next he was below the smoke, and his landing skids were inches above the water.

His hands moved automatically, centring himself, halting the descent, and then slowly drifting in a circle until he could see the indistinct finger of the old dock.

It had been eighteen years since the old helicopter had come off the assembly line. He patted the instrument panel, offered a little thank you to a God whom he had neglected since his teens and started the machine on a gentle curve towards the dock. Luckily it *was* gentle. He was no more than a hundred feet away from it when the dock itself succumbed, flashed bright flame, and sank.

His initial reaction was a quick power application, and a climb back up into the smoke again. But an experienced mind took quick control. He circled back away from the wreckage of the dock, gently felt his way downwards again, watching the altimeter spin until, again, he was under the smoke. He hung there for a minute, then pushed the microphone button. 'Charlie!' he shouted. 'I'm under the smoke level. The damn dock just blew all to hell!'

'He'll have them in the water someplace,' the answer came back. 'He's got a lot of experience. Probably north of the dock. There's deeper water up in that direction.'

'Well, how-de-do,' the pilot snorted. 'There they are, I'm making a run for the beach, Charlie. Stand by.'

'Do it good, Elmer. And be careful of Becky!'

The helicopter crabbed into the wind, making for the target group. The man among them was making signals to a place further north. The pilot took his arm directions without a quibble. Under his feather touch the old chopper approached the beach, came to a gentle halt, and settled, almost level, with its skids three feet under water. He dropped the power to idle, not daring to shut down the big power plant, and unstrapped himself.

'Which ones are going?' he shouted as he jumped out into the water.

'It's already settled,' Jake replied. 'How's your fuel load? Under a quarter?'

'Just about. Charlie Riley is worried sick about Becky.'

The man and woman turned to him at the same time.

'It's all been decided,' she said. 'Give us a hand. If we get this one on to the seat we can tie her in. Then the girl can go on the floor between the seats and we'll tie her in too.'

'Sounds good to me. Let me grab on here. God, this one is out like a light. How long will she be under?'

'If you're planning to drive down the turnpike from here to Boston at twenty miles an hour, she'll still be asleep when you arrive,' the woman chuckled at him. 'Now, Faith, you get in the middle there on the floor, there's a good girl.'

'And now we'll wrap this rope around your waist,' said Jake.

'Hey, that ain't my waist!'

'So I flunked anatomy in school. Put your legs straight out in front of you, but don't touch any of those controls. And there's a double knot to hold you in. There you go. Okay, Mr . . .?'

'Stanciewicz.'

'Okay, Mr Stanciewicz, off you go.'

'Hey, I don't know who you are!' the pilot yelled as he pulled himself into his own seat and buckled up, 'but you got a lot of guts, girl. I won't be able to come back again until this fire settles down.'

'So we'll wait,' the man said. 'Nice day for it. This smoke will raise hell with the mosquitoes, and that's all she's afraid of. Move out!'

'Yeah, sure.' The pilot grabbed with both hands for the controls.

'But what do I tell Mama?' wailed Faith.

'Tell her I've always loved her!' The noise of the chopper grew into a roar, the skids shook, the machine backed off from the shore into the middle of the lake, then shot up through the smoke and flame. When finally clear, at two thousand feet, it swept off in a gentle diving arc towards Pittsfield.

When he was sure that his machine was balanced and his passengers under reasonable control, the pilot relaxed and studied them. The woman looked like a bag of fashionable bones, so deep in sleep that she hardly moved. One towheaded little girl. Thin, of course, and sharp-boned, but a copy of Mrs Latimore if ever he had seen one. So this other one, the sleeper, must be the adopted one, the Becky that Charlie Riley was so all-fired concerned about. Elmer chuckled and pressed the microphone button.

'Latimore Operations, this is Latimore Chopper One. Mission accomplished. Two passengers aboard. One woman. One child in good shape. The woman is under some sort of sedation. And what the hell do you have to say about that, Riley!'

'Well, damn my soul, Elmer, so you really did it! Do you need to stop for medical help? If not, come all the way into Boston. The medics west of the Connecticut River are up to their necks in casualties. What did Becky have to say?'

'She didn't say nothing. She's under sedation—I told you.'

'Oh, she—I see. What about the two you left behind?'

'I didn't stand around exchanging party notes. We were pretty lucky to get out. They look like two real competent people, I wouldn't worry about them. That woman—say, she has some of the blackest hair you ever——'

'Long black hair? Why, you—what colour hair has the woman got? The one you have on board?'

'Well, sort of blonde, I guess. Dyed, maybe.'

'Why, you idiotic double-dyed sheepdip—I *told* you to be careful! That's not Becky. Let me speak to the little girl—to Faith.'

Still shaking his head at the obvious error they were making back in their safe little Operations Room, Elmer disconnected the microphone from the spare helmet under his seat and passed it along to the little girl. She seemed to know what such things were all about. She slipped it over her head, adjusted the microphone, and looked at him questioningly. On the intercom switch only he told her, 'There's Mr Riley—he's the vice-president of the company, you know. He wants to talk to you about Becky? Okay? Go ahead.' He flipped the radio switch to the talk position, and sat back to see what would happen.

The child should have been subdued, but she wasn't. 'Hi, Uncle Charlie,' she said. 'I'm sure glad you sent this helichopper. We was really in a fix, let me tell you!'

'Well. I'm glad you're out safe, Faith,' the old man's voice returned. 'Your Mom and Dad ought to be in Boston by the time you get here. That is, if the pilot can keep that thing up in the air long enough. Now tell me, how come Becky's asleep?'

'Becky? She ain't asleep, Uncle Charlie.'

'But the pilot just said she was asleep, love.'

'That's not Becky. That's Miss Mavis Pell, and, boy, is she a pain in the neck!'

'And Becky, love? Where's Becky?' There was more than a little quiver in the voice, more than a little concern.

'Oh, I thought you knew, Uncle Charlie. Becky wouldn't come. She said there wasn't enough room—that the chopper wasn't strong enough to carry us all. So she stayed back at the lake with this guy. You should see him, Uncle Charlie. What a good-lookin' guy! And I think Becky likes him a lot, let me tell you!'

He tried to direct the conversation back to where he wanted it. 'She stayed at the lake, love? Did she send a message?'

'Well, no, not really. When I asked her what I was gonna tell Mama—well, Becky just said, "Tell her that I've always loved her". Wasn't that a funny thing to say?'

There was quiet on the radio circuit. Then a younger, more impersonal voice came on. 'Latimore Helicopter One,' it said. 'You are directed to proceed to hangar four at Logan Airport. Execuflight Six and medical personnel will meet you there.'

'Yeah, well, I'll do that,' Elmer returned. 'But I want another word with Charlie—with Mr Riley.'

There was another moment of silence, and when the brisk young voice returned it was considerably subdued. 'That's not possible, Latimore One. Mr Riley has apparently suffered a heart attack. The medical team is preparing to take him to the hospital.'

CHAPTER NINE

THE two of them watched the helicopter struggle for altitude, slide away into the centre of the lake, then zoom up. For moments longer they concentrated, listening for the sound of the engine. It was almost impossible to hear anything over the orchestrated clamour of the fire. They had waded out into the lake about waist-deep. Jake pulled her closer. 'They'll make it through without a doubt,' he said cheerfully. 'Boy, what a place for a hot-dog roast.'

'If you don't mind,' retorted Becky in her quiet contralto, 'I think I'm scared enough for the two of us already! I think I could do without any more roasting jokes!'

'Feeling a little bit down in the dumps?'

'Feeling a whole lot down in the dumps,' she sighed. 'For some reason this makes the war look like a kiddie-storm.'

'Tell me about it.' He had one arm around her shoulders, and walked her out to neck-depth. His eyes constantly watched, measuring the fall of each new branch on fire, assessing the wind as the tops of lesser trees ignited.

'It wasn't even a war to begin with,' she said. 'The Society of Friends—the Quakers, you know—asked for volunteers to establish a base hospital in the north part of the country. It's almost entirely desert out there, and thousands were starving because of the drought. So I volunteered. And then a revolution broke out, and we were caught in the middle, with the Libyan army to the north of us, and the army of Chad to the south of us, and both of them being pretty careless of where their artillery shells landed. Very soon we started to get wounded from both sides, and the sick from the drought, and—well, it was a pretty bad time. But everything was organised. There was an operating tent, and separate ward tents, and an administrative tent—and everything was regular. If you didn't think of it too strongly, it seemed almost like a hospital. I wouldn't say I didn't *mind* it—with all those children—but you *could* somehow get used to it. I was due to come home after my year, when that damn mosquito bit me!'

'Made you mad, did it?' His laugh was deep and heady. She stared at him through the weaving smoke. Even under these circumstances, with ashes all over his hair, and some black streaks on his face—charcoal, probably—he looked very distinctive, and very trustworthy. She smiled back at him just as he put one hand on top of her head, shoved her underwater, and yelled 'Duck!' She gasped for breath, then heard the swish as a giant burning branch landed just where they had been standing, hissed in the water and went out.

They came up on opposite sides of the branch, spluttering. 'Isn't there supposed to be some code or warning or something?' Becky shuddered. Jake pushed the floating remnants away from them.

'There is, he said solemnly. 'You're supposed to yell "Duck" two seconds after the branch lands. Didn't I get it right?'

'Oh, you fool!' she giggled. She knew he was trying to psych her out of her fears—and it was working.

'How are you for swimming—really?' he continued. 'I know I got the wrong information the first day we met, but?'

'Oh, on a good day I guess I could make a mile, or maybe a mile and a half,' she allowed. 'And on scared days I could go three. And this is one of my scared days. What are you looking at?'

He waved his hand generally towards the hill where his

low cabin still stood intact. 'That ought to be about our fireline,' he said calmly. 'It's not really the fire or the debris we need to worry about, it's the smoke. Once the flame hits my cabin, things will start reaching out as far as we are now.'

'And then?'

'And then we'll take a little swim. The best bet, for the moment, is that other side of the island.'

'But that won't last long as a refuge, will it?'

'No, not very. It won't take long for the fire to jump the narrow part of the channel, and then we have to play ducks and drakes with the island.'

'I—I guess I don't fully understand, Mr Meadows. I'll have to depend on you.'

'Well then, dear lord, don't call me Mr Meadows,' he laughed. 'Jake is the name. Jake. Come on, now, don't lose your sense of humour.'

'I—I don't feel much like laughing,' she sighed. 'I've got this feeling that everything has drained out of me—everything. Is that the way it is, when you're on your last road?'

'You don't really have to laugh,' he chuckled, 'but you and I are so far from the last road that *that's* funny. Make a little small talk.'

'And then we'll swim a while?'

'Right, and talk some more. Tell me some more about the Latimores.'

'The way you say that I know you mean about the crazy Latimores, don't you?'

'Hey, I didn't say that! The little lady I met on the first day—Mary Kate? What about her?'

'Mary Kate? That's her name, of course, but only Pop calls her that. My brother and I, we always call her Ma. That's my older brother. You don't know him. He's the farmer. He and Anna have the family farm, and they have four children now and—oh, Henry is a Chase, not a Latimore. I used to be a Chase, and Ma did, too.'

'Your Ma was a lawyer?'

'Oh, sure, now she is. But in October she gets to be a judge in the Superior Court. But that's only now, and because the doctor, he said she might not have any more children. Well, when I first knew Mary Kate she was my mother, a farmer's wife, a law student, a lady who could do anything that a kid needed. You know the kind?'

'A mother you could go crying to?'

'Always a sympathetic shoulder, Mary Kate had, but you'd better be right in your argument, believe me.'

'Oh! That's a different kind. A real toughie with a paddle?'

'No!' Becky's exasperation showed him that she was entirely bound up in the past, and had almost forgotten the fire. Which had been his point all along. 'No! You'll never get it right, Jake. In all my life, Ma has corrected me a lot of times, but has never ever laid a hand on me. Not ever. You'll just have to meet Mary Kate and talk to her.'

And wouldn't that be nice? she told herself. If Jake and I could know each other for years, and Ma would have time to approve of him, and Pop could give him the once-over! What the devil do *I* know about men? Except that I trust him, and I—and I don't know what else. What did Pop say? 'Your mother and I are in love because we complement each other. She has strengths where I have weaknesses, and vice versa. We've arrived at compromise all through our married life. Sure, there's a form of domination in our family. In my own field, I dominate your mother; in hers, she's the ruler.'

Jake broke in on her thoughts. 'Hey, little lady, talk's over. It's time for swimming. The flame just came past our fireline.'

He turned over on his stomach very slowly and watched critically as she began a smooth and easy breast-stroke. Evidently satisfied with her performance, he rolled over on his back again to check the progress of the fire, then came up behind her in an effortless Australian crawl. His strokes were things of beauty—effortless, yet powerful. Becky did her best to match his speed, then grinned at him as she gave up the race and fell back on her basic stroke. He immediately slowed.

Once or twice he came close to give some directions. It was easy enough to see what he was about. The island lay close by them—too close for its dry jungle to escape the eventual spark. The creosote-loaded tree-trunks on the mainland were exploding, throwing out great clumps of burning debris.

They were approaching the island in a wide arc so that, while it stood unburned, it served as a sort of firebreak for them. And Jake was swimming cautiously, with his eyes on the sky. Twice he came vaulting over her, forcing her down to the bottom of the lake, as stray embers boomed loose from the mainland and splattered far out into the lake. The wind was rising, propelling the wreckage ever closer to them.

It seemed like hours, but could only have been minutes, before he rolled over on his back, floating, and called for a break. Becky joined him quickly. Her muscles were complaining; they had not yet recovered fully from the strains of malaria, and, besides, she could feel the chill of fear creeping up her spine again.

'Take a break here,' he called over to her, voice as calm as if he had been escorting her on a walk though Boston Common.

'Sure,' she puffed, hoping she wasn't giving away as much of her weakness as it seemed. They were in the lee of the island now, and except for the firepeaks all around the lake, and the rolling clouds of smoke, one might almost think things were normal. Keep saying that, she chided herself. Keep up your courage. Look at him, he's not worried. Lord, if Dante could have seen something like this, he would never have depicted Hell as a place of ice! This is it, right here, right now, and strangely, I'm—

I'm what? I'm not glad to be *here*, I'm just glad to be with him.

Look at him! He seemed to be swimming aimlessly around, diving out of sight once or twice, and then suddenly he stopped swimming and was standing up. 'Over here,' he called. Becky went willingly.

'I knew there was a sandbar somewhere out in this area.' Jake reached out his hands to bring her close. The water that sloped off his shoulders was over her head. She made a couple of attempts to touch bottom, and then gave up as one of his arms swept her up against his shoulder. 'Just hang on there,' he ordered. She put both hands up on his shoulders, then rested her chin there. For some reason she felt—well, perhaps not comfortable, but at least safe.

'Isn't it strange,' she suggested when she had caught her breath, 'how simple life is when you come right down to it.'

'Simple?'

'Well, uncomplicated. I just hope that—well, I know Ma will worry. She's always been a secret worrier. And Pop, too. He's a wonderful man, my father. Of course he isn't really my father— he's my adoptive father. Strange, it's been ten years now, and I hardly think of him that way. How about your family? Your mother and sisters?'

'My mother remarried, and they live down in Florida. I see them from time to time, not too often. One sister lives in California. I get a yearly Christmas card, but I don't believe I've seen her in, oh—two years or more. The other sister married a diplomat and they travel all over the world, so I don't see too much of them either.'

'Oh, Jake, that's awful!' she exclaimed. 'You just don't know, do you!'

'Know what?'

'Know what it means to be surrounded by people who love you, and whom you love in return. I'd be lost if I didn't know that Ma and Pop are out doing something for us right now. Or maybe Henry is, too—my brother, you know—or even Mattie. And Uncle Charlie for sure. All of them helping. And you, too, dear Jake!'

'All of them?' He laughed, a quiet little doubting laugh. 'I'd feel a lot better about it knowing that *I* was doing something about it. You're a nice kid, doctor, but that isn't the way you get things done in this rough world. You have to fend for yourself. Have you ever heard the one about "he travels fastest who travels alone"?'

'That's great if you want to set a new world speed record,' Becky sighed. There were cold fingers clutching at her heart again. Alone. He wanted to be alone when we arrived here. Does he *still* feel the same way? Put a good face on it all. Make a joke. Do something. She looked at her waterproof wristwatch, Pop's gift to her when she graduated from college. 'I'll bet you right now—it's three-thirty in the afternoon—I'll bet you ten dollars that right now Pop is getting everything in gear to come and get us!'

'Say, I'd be sure to lose,' laughed Jake. 'My damn watch has stopped. Duck, here comes another visitor!'

Another twenty minutes passed before they were safely out of the way of the new outbreak. 'We've about run out of luck here,' he said when they surfaced behind the drifting branches that had almost caught them on the surface. 'It's all burning down the hill now, and starting to jump to the island.'

For a moment Becky closed her eyes and rested her head on his shoulder. Then she shook herself, cleared her hair from her eyes, and said, 'Okay, what do we do next?'

'Come on, lady, as fast as you can make it!'

He was gone, sunk and away from her before she caught up to the conversation. She dog-paddled for a second, then took out after him with her own version of the crawl. It was clumsy, wasted a great deal of her slender budget of strength, but for a brief time it moved her along the water at speed.

He was already there when she arrived, resting his elbows on the flat bottom of an overturned rowboat. His hand grabbed her just as she ran out of power. 'Hang on here,' he gasped at her. 'If this isn't luck!'

'Lucky, hell!' she snapped at him. 'Now what do we do?'

He stared at her for a startled moment, then shrugged his shoulders. 'It's low in the water,' he told her, 'and as wet as we can ask for. What we're going to do is to push her, just the way she is, around the corner of the island. If we can get past Salter's Point there, the wind will be blowing away from us, and we can just sit there nice and cosy until help comes, or until we turn into fish, or whatever. Give a hand.'

Becky took the easiest part of the job, hanging on to the stern and kicking. He went up forward and tried to drag at the craft. Once it was moving in the right direction, he came back to the stern beside her. Twice, at his alarm, they dived underwater and came up in the little pocket of air trapped under the boat, while whizzing balls of flame were hurled at them, like mortar shells, from the island.

It was tiring, all of it, and Becky had not been strong when she came to the little mountain resort. She tried to hide her problem, and each time Jake came to the stern to check on her progress she made sure she was kicking away with all her strength. Until the last time, when he lazily paced himself around the boat and started to say, 'Becky, we're really making progress. Just a few more yards and——' He stopped. Because Becky was not kicking away at her accustomed position, draped across the pintle of the rudder. Time and trouble had caught up with her, and Becky Latimore trailed the boat by a good ten feet, her head down in the water, and with no movement of her feet.

'Oh, God,' he gasped, 'Becky!' He covered the distance in two massive racing strokes, trailed her over on her back, and struck out doggedly for the swamped rowboat. It took superhuman strength to heave her up on to the flat bottom of the boat. Disregarding his own bruises, he spread her out flat on her back, checked to be sure she had not swallowed her tongue, and began the kiss of life.

Embers were still shooting down at them from the island. Those that were only close, he ignored; those that were on target he knocked away with a tremendous smash of his forearm. And all the while he forced air down into her lungs, let it exhaust, forced more air in, let it exhaust—and at long last there was a strangled movement as the girl began to breathe. She rolled over on her side and vomited most of the water she had swallowed, breathed again, haphazardly at first, and then with a long sigh she began to breathe regularly, fully.

Jake squatted near her feet. The terrible tension in his face was still there, and it held until she finally made a noise. He vaulted in one movement to her head. 'Becky,' he pleaded.

'I'm—I'm all right,' she said softly. 'I'm all right, Jake. One very weak hand slid along the wooden strakes of the boat and touched his hand. His own hesitated for a moment, then surrounded her long slender fingers in his huge hand. 'Thank God,' he told her. They sat in silence for a time, he still guarding against embers, she merely resting and drawing strength from him.

'Becky,' he said, 'I have to make a confession.'

'We all do, sooner or later,' she whispered. 'Go ahead.'

'It's about you and Mavis,' he sighed. 'She was hunting me, so I had to get rid of her. I didn't believe in marriage, so I played around with you to make her give up.'

'And that's the confession?' she sighed. 'You needn't have done that, Jake. It was the outdoor life that turned her off. And I knew what you were up to all the time. Don't let it worry you.'

Becky could see the sense of relief that flooded his face. It was a terrible struggle for her, but, tired and worn as she was, he saw no indication in *her* face that she was crying inside. More quickly than she knew, Doctor Rebecca Latimore had switched her priorities in the last few days, away from science and test tubes and famous operations to small cottages, children, and a man who came home to them every day. This rugged man, lying beside her on the wet straking of the overturned boat— he was just the one she could want. When the tears finally broke through, he ascribed it to the influx of smoke, billowing gagging smoke, that drove them both off the top of the boat, and down under, where the stale air bubble still supported the crumbling structure.

When they came back out, things looked more clear, and Becky had regained control of her wildly spinning emotions. I need time to think, to plan, she told herself. It all hurt. Jake was a loner. He didn't believe in marriage. And so there would be no children around the cottage— at least none of hers. A cottage, and maybe a couple of cats? But no other man. Not after knowing Jake. She was so engrossed in her own thoughts, and he was busy at the bow, when a tiny branch, no more than two inches in diameter, and perhaps four feet long, wheeled out at them from the island. It glanced off Becky's head—not hard enough to do any damage, she thought, until he yelled and swam towards her. It wasn't until he started beating at her head, forcing her underwater, that she realised that her long black hair had burst into flames. She came up, struggling for breath. The raven locks were gone—not entirely, but enough to create havoc. What was left hung in two scattered and frail links on either side of her face.

'Damn! Damn!' muttered Jake. 'Does it hurt?'

'No!' she cried. He could tell she was lying, but what he did *not* know was that she was crying for her lost vanity, for her lost pride, for her lost love. He held her close as the tears fell, without knowing that he was prolonging the problem, rather than helping. It was then that they both saw the pair of bobcats swimming towards them from the island.

'They're only looking for a place to hide,' she cried at him. 'They deserve a place too. They won't hurt us.'

'You read too many fool books,' he snarled. 'Sure they're looking for a place to hide. And certainly they won't hurt us—unless we get in the way of their own safety. There's only one boat out here. Just where the hell do you think they're heading? And they're already scared, so just what the hell do you think they'll do? I know they look small and lovable, woman, but they're not, and we're in no position for a fight. Come on!'

She went reluctantly, too tired, too depressed, to really care any more. She wanted to tell him that she didn't care what the bobcats might do to them. She really didn't care. But as soon as they had cleared the boat, he could see without being told. She was too far gone in her depression to fight back as he flipped her over on her back, got one hand securely under her chin, and started off with a side stroke for the mainland.

She was unconscious but breathing when he brought her into shallow water, almost exactly in the place where they had started. The heat of the flame, the strength of the wind, had kindled and then cooled the area around the beach, and by careful movement Jake was able to bring her up on to the sand, half in and half out of the water. He checked her breathing carefully, made her as comfortable as possible and sat down beside her. For the first time he noticed the huge burn that enveloped his right upper arm and shoulder. He shrugged his shoulders, and settled down to let luck run its last course.

The situation at Boston's Logan airport was more than a little confusing. The battle against fire was being conducted over a hundred miles away, at the furthest extremity of the state. And yet at Logan Airport two fire-related 'Mayday' landings were under way. The first had been expected. A cranky old Sikorsky helicopter had announced itself more than ten minutes earlier. Two ambulances and a fire truck stood by at the parking area in front of hangar four. Controllers on duty, familiar with the old ark, were keeping a weather eye open on the western approaches.

The second, however, had surprised everybody. An executive jet was scheduled in from Bermuda. It had made record time, and there had been a great deal of radio traffic from the plane to the downtown operations centre of the huge construction company. Routinely, the controllers had assigned it to position number six among the aircraft waiting to land. And then, out of a clear blue sky, the pilot of the executive jet had broken in on the air control channel with the sort of message no controller wants to hear. 'Mayday, Mayday, this is Latimore Execuflight Six. Flameout!'.

There had been a moment or two of furore in the tower, but quickly enough the craft was cleared to land as first priority. In the bustle and confusion, no one on the ground stopped to ask themselves how *both* jet engines on that aircraft could have flamed out at the same time. The plane let down nicely, making for all the world like a perfectly normal descent, and the engines seemed to have re-fired, for the pilot waved off the land tug sent out to meet it. It, too, taxied up to the landing pad of the Latimore hangar area, and things returned to normal in the busy control tower. Within six months, they knew, some pilot would be asked to explain it all, but that was paperwork — something you worried about on long lonely nights when nobody was flying.

Down at the hangar, however, a perturbed Bruce Latimore was having a word or two with his tiny wife. 'Damn, you can't do things that way, Mary Kate! We could have interrupted some *real* emergency. I could lose my pilot's licence.'

'Look at that helicopter,' she retorted. 'It looks old enough to be in the Fourth of July parade. Stop this stupid airplane, Bruce. Now, please!'

'Mary Kate, I can't do impossible things. Cool down! We'll be there in just a minute.' He gave her a fondly patient look, and found himself glaring at a faceful of feminine emotions which were about to explode. 'Bruce Latimore,' she shouted at him above the jet noises, 'for over ten years I've bowed and scraped and nursemaided you—but those are my children out there! And I'm not going to sit here waiting for you to follow instructions. *Now*, Bruce!'

'Be reasonable, Mary Kate. They're my kids too!'

'I'm being reasonable, Bruce. You'll like sleeping on the couch in the living-room!'

Which covered about all the argument Bruce Latimore cared to make. The jet's brakes squealed, and it jerked to a squeaky stop about forty feet from the old helicopter. A trio of paramedics were busy unstrapping Mavis Pell from the seat of the machine. As soon as the steps to the jet were unfolded, the tiny figure of Mary Kate was on the taxiway, running desperately towards the helicopter.

'Lookit! What did I tell you?' Faith announced grandly as the ground-crew struggled with the ropes that tied her in. 'That's my mama!'

'Don't be in such a hurry,' the usually taciturn pilot said. 'Your father still has to park that aircraft.' Nevertheless, the jet was still moving down the tarmac when Faith bolted and ran for her mother.

'Now, what the hell did they give this chick?' The paramedics were trying to pressure the helicopter pilot to commit himself.

'I dunno,' Elmer responded. 'She was having hysterics or something. The doc tied a tag to her wrist.'

'Here,' the third member of the trio reported, 'we don't

gotta rush with this babe, fellers. She'll be asleep for a lot of hours.'

'Well, get her out of my chopper,' gruffed Elmer. 'I don't know what the hell's going on, but for sure I gotta go somewhere else.' He reached for the ignition, but Mary Kate was on him before he could get the engine started.

'Elmer! Where's my Becky? You left my Becky back in that firestorm?'

'I didn't have no choice, Mrs Mary. By the time I got there, she'd already decided who was goin' where. I give her some lip, and she tells me to shove off. What could I do?'

'Nothing, Elmer, nothing. Becky's almost as pig-headed as her——. Tell me, will this pile of scrap iron take us back?'

'Well, it ain't the fastest thing ever rode down the 'pike. And the engine sounds like it needs a major operation.'

'Is there anything else around here that will fly?'

'Now, Mrs Mary, I don't want to get caught up in no wild schemes—I mean, no *more* wild schemes today. But if you was to look down the line there, ain't that the new seaplane that the Corporation bought two weeks ago? Now that would be speedy, for sure, only——'

'Only what?'

'Only I ain't too sure we could get it down. It's a chance. If that smoke has cleared, so we could see an approach—well, there we'd be, wouldn't we?'

'And what's the chance, Elmer?'

'You're asking me, Mrs Latimore?'

'I'm asking you, Elmer. Charlie Riley told me you were the best pilot in the Corporation. Well?'

'Well—oh, my God, Mrs Latimore! Mr Riley, he got all that excited when he heard the report, he had a heart attack!'

'Yes, I know. We talked to Operations while we were landing. They've got him into Massachusetts General and—there are just too many things to do, aren't there! Just let me sit here and think for a minute.' Mary Kate plumped herself down on the skidbrace of the helicopter and concentrated. Her husband was making his way out of the jet. Faith saw him first, and ran.

'Hey, little lady!' he chuckled as he tossed her up in the air and twirled her around. 'What's wrong?'

His nine-year-old daughter summed it all up from her own perspective. 'Becky couldn't come with us, and Mama is crying, and Uncle Charlie is sick.'

'Yes, I know.' He did his best to cheer the child up, then carried her in his arms over to the helicopter, and crowded down on the strut beside his wife. Mary Kate looked up at him for a moment, then nodded her head.

She leaned against his capacious shoulder, and his arm automatically came around to comfort her. 'I don't know why it is,' she sighed. 'I love them all—one as much as another—but when something happens to Becky—I just can't stand up to it, Bruce, I just can't!'

'It's because she will always be our first,' he said.

'We'll get her out, Bruce?'

'Of course we will, Mary Kate.'

'I've got an idea!' Her eyes sparkled at the thought. He shuddered. 'No, Mary Kate,' he hastened to squeeze in. 'You get to take care of Faith. You also get to go and see how Charlie Riley is making out.'

'While you go after Becky?'

'Don't rock the boat, love,' he returned. 'We're not going to do this in a rush. We've got to plan. It's the only sensible way to do.'

'I don't want to be sensible, Bruce, I want to go and get Becky. She's my—my trust. I *have* to go and get her!'

'Come on,' he comforted. 'It takes a plan. Now, you get on your way to the hospital. Elmer can drive you. I'll get over to the Operations Centre and get a hand on things. Right?'

It wasn't until he had waved them off in the limousine that he remembered to whom he had been talking. 'If you say so, Bruce.' Hah! Like a snake-oil salesman at the County Fair! But the car was already out of sight, and beyond his control. He shrugged his shoulders, hoped for the best, and slid into the second limousine that had whispered around the corner of the hangar. 'Operations Centre,' he ordered, then sat back to think.

The trip from the airport to downtown Boston was its usual trial. It was almost five o'clock when he finally stepped out of the elevator and was ushered into the dimly-lit Operations Room. The senior programmer, a man of about forty, came hurrying up to report. Bruce waved him aside and read the boards.

'Charlie Riley is in stable condition?'

'Yes, sir. That report is thirty minutes old. The doctor said he was conscious but deeply troubled until he talked to your wife. That seemed to improve him immensely.'

'Good, good. Now, what's our position with helicopters in the western part of the state?'

'Two six-passengers will be released by the State Police in about two hours, sir. They're prepared to turn them over to us at Northampton.

'Northampton? They have an all-weather airport there, don't they?'

'Yes, sir.'

'And what's the report from Lake Mohawk?'

'The fires are still burning around the perimeter of the lake, sir. There's still a heavy blanket of smoke in the area. Visibility is practically nil.'

'But Elmer got in there earlier, didn't he?'

'Yes, sir, but you know how *he* flies.'

'Yes, I do, young man. I've flown with him for years.' There was a coldness in his voice that reduced a considerable part of the programmer's enjoyment.

'Yes, sir,' he said, and waited.

The orders weren't long in coming. 'I want both the helicopters to Northampton,' ordered Bruce. 'Refuelled, refitted, and held until I get there. A twin-engine from Logan within—oh, let's say thirty minutes. To take Elmer and me to Northampton. A call to my wife now, so I can tell her what's up.' He turned away from the young man and stared out of the window, waiting. Waiting. It was not something he did gracefully, had never done it at all, to be truthful about it, until he met and married Mary Kate Chase. The memory brushed his mind. Love me, love my daughter—that had been Mary Kate's laughing statement the night he proposed to her. Love me, love my Becky. Damn!

The voice at his elbow was hesitant. 'Mr Latimore—we—can't seem to reach your wife at the hospital. The attendant says that she spoke briefly to Mr Riley, and when he went to sleep, she left.'

Bruce waved his hand vaguely, but something was itching at him in a place he couldn't scratch. 'Probably gone home,' he commented, without looking around. 'Look, just in case, see if you can get me Mr or Mrs Henry Chase, in Eastboro. My stepson. The number's sure to be in the computer.'

Back to the seagulls again. Strange how they followed the flight paths between the tall buildings, and then occasionally took a wild fling at the craggy tops. The voice at his side again. 'Mr Chase,' the young man said nervously. 'Mr Henry Chase.'

'Hello, Henry? This is Bruce.' It seemed hardly worth calling your stepson by something other than his name, considering that he was only five years younger than you were, and more than once had threatened to punch you in the mouth!

'Yes, Bruce. You stirring up some fuss or something? Mary Kate talked to Anna about forty minutes ago, and now my wife has zoomed out of here without a word, leaving me all alone with my own kids—and two of yours, too.'

'Say that again, slowly, Henry. Mary Kate is not there. And Anna is not there. What the hell is going on?'

'Hey, you married her!' the younger man chuckled. 'She was a perfectly good stepmother, and you had to up and marry her. Now, as far as I know about the plot for the day, my wife has taken my best car to drive up to the Hilton. That's in Boston, you'll remember. Where she's going to pick up one more of your children and bring her back down here to wait for further instructions. Now it's your turn.'

'Henry, I swear one of these days I'm going to—no I'm not, either. I tried that once, and it took months to recover from it. I haven't the slightest idea what's going on. Except for Becky. You heard about Becky?'

'I heard. And if you were to guess, what would you suppose Mary Kate is up to now?'

'Henry, I still don't know. But if some idea flashes across your mind, you'd . . . damn! She wouldn't *dare* do that. I'll call you some time, Henry. G'bye.'

Bruce's eyes were sparking as he slammed the telephone down and turned to his assistant. 'In words of one syllable,' he instructed the young man, 'what other vehicle or aircraft of ours has unexpectedly moved in the last two hours?'

The young man shuddered. It would make a great story for the day after tomorrow, how he and the boss had established a rescue plan, but just at this moment he was shaking in his shoes as he queried the computer.

Numbers flashed up on the screen. The Latimore Construction Corporation, doing business all over the world, maintained an air force of its own, somewhat bigger than most countries in South America. One by one their numbers flashed on the screen, waited for the required twenty reading seconds, and flashed off. On and off, green against black, curious aeroplane names, stranger destinations. 'Whoa! That one,' Bruce Latimore indicated. The computer operator stopped the flow, backed up one appearance, and let the information stand.

'Cessna 16782, from Boston Harbor station. No flight plan filed.'

'Hit it again,' he ordered. 'What's so unusual about Cessna 16782?'

The buttons moved again, the machine ruminated, and the answer flashed on the wall as Bruce Latimore slammed his massive fist into the table in front of him. The screen said, 'Cessna 16782, equipped for water transport and rescue. Pontoons. Side-looking radar. Ordered to flight by Mrs Mary Kate Latimore. Pilot, Mr Elmer Stanciewicz.'

'Great heaven!' muttered Bruce, coming back out of his chair as if the springs had had their strength redoubled. 'How long ago?'

'Almost one——' and the operator suddenly remembered that you never said 'almost' to Bruce Latimore. 'Fifty-nine minutes,' he corrected himself, 'and thirty-nine seconds!'

The chief of the Latimore Corporation tapped his fingers on the table, rattling all the accumulated papers. 'How soon can you get me airborne?'

The young man consulted his watch, ignoring the dozens of clocks scattered around the room. 'The plane is ready now, sir. The question is, how soon can we get you to Logan. The evening rush hour has already started.'

'All right, I'll start at once,' he ordered. 'Alert the plane. And find me another pilot.' He got up from his chair, stretched, and took a step or two. And then he did the thing that endeared him to all his huge corporation.

'Henzman,' he mused, shaking his head slowly, 'I don't know of any worse combination than an Irish wife and a Polish pilot. Avoid them if you can!' He clapped the young man on the shoulder and made for the door.

CHAPTER TEN

BECKY leaned back in the sand in a fit of lethargy. After all the excitement, nothing seemed to matter any more. Jake lay beside her, not more than five feet away, and said nothing.

Strange, she told herself wearily. I've lost half my blouse, most of my denims. Jake wasn't wearing much to begin with—just a pair of frayed shorts. And here we lie, Adam and Eve. Her eyes wandered. The flames on their side of the lake were considerably reduced, although the rest of the rim of cliffs still blazed in unconstrained fury. Smoke whirled around them. She lifted the water-soaked cloth, part of her missing blouse, to cover her eyes and nose. Jake made not a move. He must be tired to the bone, she thought. I am, too. He doesn't recognise that I'm a woman. Here I am, half naked. It doesn't bother me, and he doesn't even notice. Is it because I'm so tired? Because we've been to the edge of life? Maybe some day, wherever we are, we'll both sit back and think about it, and laugh? Or cry, perhaps. Because wherever that is, we won't be together. He's not ready for marriage, remember? And I'm not ready for anything less!

She sat up, crossing her legs and staring out over the lake. The smoke cloud had risen to almost a hundred feet, and it was possible to see more than halfway across to the other shore. That pair of bobcats had abandoned the boat, and they were now swimming back to the island. Always in pairs? Everything moved into the Ark, two by two? Just ahead of her a single raccoon broke from cover and ruined the theory. She crumbled a bit of branch in her hands—all that remained unburnt within fifty yards—and threw it at the water. It made a most satisfactory plop. Across the lake there was a dull boom as a particularly large tree burst into flame. Now that the fire had bypassed them it had become interesting instead of fearsome.

'Jake?' she offered. After a time, he rolled in her direction and grunted.

'You saved my life, Jake.' Not a thank you, just an ordinary statement of fact. He grunted again.

'Jake, you know an awful lot about staying alive in difficult conditions. How come?'

He yawned at her. Without staring, it was hard to tell whether it was real or artificial, that yawn. 'How come?' she insisted.

'Oh, when I was younger I was assigned to a special outfit in the army. A special forces unit, which specialised in survival. It was a long time ago, but you don't forget.'

'And is that what your book is about? Survival?'

'Hell, no,' he grunted. He started to roll over on his side, away from her.

'Jake,' she insisted, 'I've got to talk to somebody, or go out of my mind!' He shifted around again.

'No need to do that,' he said. 'I don't remember when I've seen a woman handle herself as well as you. We had a saying in the Army that you never really understand a guy until you've seen him shot at a few times. You've passed your baptism of fire, Becky Latimore. But if you want to talk, I'm listening.'

Now that she had his attention she turned shy, pulling her knees up against her breasts, and wrapping her arms protectively around them. 'I—I'm thankful for what you've done,' she murmured. God, how do you offer yourself to a man! 'Very thankful. I'm willing to—to do whatever you want in repayment. Anything.'

'Yes, there *is* something you can do for me,' he laughed.

The laughter startled her, made her jump. But she was

determined. 'Anything,' she repeated. 'Name it.'

'Well, Doc,' he said, 'I think I've burned the hell out of my arm and shoulder. Would you mind taking a look?'

Oh, God, she thought, as she forced her weary body up and moved over to him. I thought—he—and then she drew in her breath in astonishment. The blisters on his shoulder were more than two inches in diameter. Those on his upper arm, where he had batted away the flaring ingots, had already broken, and were inflamed. 'My God,' she sighed. 'And I've lost my bag!'

'Not to worry,' he chuckled. Becky stared at him in amazement. With all the pain there must be associated with that burn, and still he laughed? He sat up and looked around. How *can* he do it? she asked herself. Lord, thank you for leaving *this* man to watch over me.

'Down there,' he pointed. 'Water-lilies, underwater-growths—anything like that. Make a pad of it.'

'Yes, of course.' Her body rebelled, but she forced it to go on. The two hundred feet down the beach might as well have been miles, but she made it. She crushed the water-growths gently. They were not sanitary, like the salt-water plants, but they were something. Her fumbling hands took longer than necessary to make poultices, but tying them on? 'Don't look,' she laughed at Jake as she tore up the remainder of her blouse and used the cloth for ties, for pads.

'Oh, I won't,' he promised, and didn't. The work took over half an hour, but they seemed to offer him some comfort. When she was finished she gently dropped a kiss on the top of his head and knelt down in the sand beside him.

'Look at you,' he commented. 'We've ruined your beautiful hair.' It was the first time Becky had noticed since the incident occurred. She ran her hands gently through what remained, wincing at the few bare spots on the top of her head. 'And I forgot my make-up case, too,' she giggled, trying to make a joke of it all. She *had* to do it or fall back into depression, into hysteria!

'Watch still running?' He was resolutely facing away from her.

'Yeah,' she commented. 'Ought to be. My dad paid a fortune for the thing. Almost six o'clock.'

'Oh, your *dad* paid a mint for it!'

'Did I miss something there? It was my graduation present.'

'No, you didn't miss anything,' he said softly. 'Six o'clock? Where's your mother?'

'Where's my mother? Oh, you mean about that bet. Well, don't sell us Latimore women short, wise guy. There's still a couple of hours until twilight.'

'I'm not rushing you,' he chuckled. 'I figure that bet is a sure thing. For me, that is. Don't look like anyone's coming in here by air tonight. Maybe tomorrow.'

'Yes,' she sighed, 'maybe tomorrow.' There was a moment of silence. 'Jake?'

'Yeah?'

'I know it's personal and all, but—did you—are you . . .'

'Married? Not me. You?'

'I—no.'

'How come, a pretty girl like you?'

'Me? Come on, now! You should see my sister Mattie!'

'Jealous, are you?'

Becky flared up at that. 'Never!' she snapped. 'Envious, maybe, but not jealous. Mattie and I always share—always. After all, she lent me her father! Maybe that's why I haven't got married.'

'Because you have a stepfather? That's stupid!'

'Not that,' she giggled. 'Not ever that. No, really, every time I look at some guy—you know, like people do, and say *hey, is he the one*? Well, every time I do that I end up comparing him to Pop.'

'And down the drain he goes?'

'I—if I got married, I'd have to see him every day, and

count on him, and trust him. I want a man who'll make me as happy as Pop has made my mother.'

'And "them kind" is pretty scarce on the shore, huh?'

She almost said it. 'They don't make that kind of man any more.' It almost got out, until her senses took over and shut her mouth. Why would I say that? she asked herself. There must be plenty more made like Pop. Why, here's one sitting next to me right now!

'You ever thought of getting married, Jake?' she asked.

'Thought about it, sure. But decided against it pretty quickly. After all, why should I make one woman miserable when I can spread myself around amongst a whole crowd of them?'

'Modesty doesn't run in your family, I take it?'

'Perhaps not.' He was still staring at the distant hills, carefully avoiding her half-nude figure.

'I can see how a girl could fall in love with you very quickly, Jake.' That jerked him around to stare at her.

'Any girl?'

'Well, almost any girl. Present company excepted, of course.'

'Ah, of course. You're dedicated to the surgical theatre, right? Cut them bones, lift them ribs, for the good of humanity and a hundred thousand dollars a year!'

'Don't mock me!' she snarled at him. 'It's not the money. I don't need the damn money!'

'Oh? Own fifty per cent of the Latimore Construction empire, do you?'

'No!' she snarled, wanting to hurt him. 'Only five per cent. Two and a half, really. Mattie and I share that too.'

'Well!' That seemed to shut him up, but that wasn't what she wanted, not at this point! One of the pads on his shoulder was coming loose. She repositioned the rags to hold it more firmly in place, and then found herself unable to remove her fingers. They slipped to the edge of the pad, touched lightly on his burned skin, and stayed there. Not for all the tea in wherever could she get them to move. It didn't seem to bother him. He was doing some heavy thinking, his brow all wrinkled and his lips moving regularly in and out, in and out.

'Becky,' he said at last. 'There's something about war that women, thank God, never have to learn.'

She looked at him but said nothing. Of course women had nothing to learn from war. They only have to sit home and worry and fight the world, and ponder the futility of it all!

'When you go into combat,' he continued, 'you go as a team. Very suddenly a person whom you've never known before becomes the guarantor of your life.'

'And?' She knew what he was describing. The fellowship of combat veterans. When death stood at their side and choices were madly indiscriminate, there was left a bond closer than anything else in the world.

He seemed to be choosing words carefully. 'It's something that happens the first time, or never happens at all,' he murmured. 'But——'

'But?'

'But I never thought it could happen between a man and a woman!'

'Between a man and a——?' Whatever her question had been, there was no place or time to ask it. Out of the rolling clouds of smoke to the north a gleaming red and white aircraft had dived under the smoke, over the firestorm, and was making a pass almost directly over their heads. The wings waggled, the plane pulled up, and vanished into the smoke again.

'What was that?' asked Becky, feeling as stupid as she looked.

'Beats me,' Jake laughed. 'It might have been an eagle or a condor—except that it had LATIMORE CON-STRUCTION printed on the side in big letters. Your mother's come for us?'

'Don't be silly,' she snapped. 'We have over fifty pilots. My mother can't fly worth beans. Dad tried to teach her, Mattie tried to teach her, I tried to teach her—nothing! They'll come back, won't they?' And that's as heavy a bit of wishful thinking as any fool could make, she told herself.

Jake wasn't laughing. 'They'll be back,' he comforted her, slipping one arm around her shoulders. 'Listen!'

The sound was returning, but by this time it was obvious that the aircraft had slowed down. The engine snarled and burped a couple of times and then there it was, at the furthest end of the lake, swaying and dodging and bouncing just below the smoke banks.

'My God,' groaned Jake. 'Pontoons! They're going to try to land in the lake! Idiots!'

'What's so idiotic about that?' she flared at him. 'That's what pontoons are for!'

'No wonder you couldn't teach your mother to fly,' he snapped. 'The lake is full of junk and debris. Look at that damn fool put that thing down! You'd think he was landing on a millpond. Smooth! Like a baby's——'

'Don't hold back,' she snapped, 'I've heard that expression before. And I suggest an apology is in order, Mr Meadows.'

'It sure will be if they can make it all the way across the lake,' he snorted. 'Come on, baby, coax it a little more, there's the good guy! What the hell is he tail-fishing for?'

The 'why' became very evident. The plane was trying to dodge something. It was about a hundred yards from them—one football field's worth, and running parallel to the shoreline of the little lake. They heard the noise first—a crumbling sound, as the craft caught one pontoon on some obstruction, swung in a half-circle, and came to a dead stop, engine off, and only the navigational lights flashing at them.

Almost immediately the plane began to sink by the nose, tilting further and further as the damaged pontoon

filled, and the weight of the water pulled it inexorably
down.

Jake struggled to his feet. 'Now if the damn fools only
have the sense to——' Becky managed to get up with
him. They heard the tremendous sigh as the plane's cabin
door popped open. An orange rubber life-raft hit the
water and began to inflate. A few isolated packages were
thrown out from the cockpit into the raft. A man
scrambled down into the bouncing float and held it
steady while a tiny graceful feminine figure stepped
daintily from the step in the wing and into the boat,
without ruffling a hair, it seemed. The man began to
paddle. Becky reached out one hand to stop Jake.

'Save your breath,' she giggled almost hysterically.
'Now's where I say, "I told you so". It's——' she stopped
to consult her watch, '—it's twenty minutes past seven,
Mr Meadows, and you might as well sit down and wait.
The Marines have landed! At any rate, Elmer and my
mother have!'

An hour later they were all gathered around the little
fire that Elmer had scraped together for warmth. The
summer night was getting cold. The fringes of the forest
fire, high on the opposing cliffs, were flickering out.
Becky checked Jake's pads one more time. The new ones,
of course. Her mother had made sure that the first thing
out of the plane was the extra-large medical rescue kit.
Wet sanitised pads had replaced his floral decorations,
and a saline bag stood ready just in case. The moment the
raft had grounded on the shore, Becky had thrown
herself at her mother, towering over her, but feeling so
slight and small beside this woman she worshipped. 'Oh,
Ma!' she cried, and then again, 'oh, Ma!'

'It's been a long trip, Becky. But you are well? Why is it
that every time I see you with this man you don't seem to
have any clothes on?'

'It's a long story,' Becky returned.

'Then before you tell it, put this on,' her mother

insisted. 'I don't know *why* I brought a raincoat, but I did. Now, the story.'

The gathering darkness helped to hide Becky's blushes, and the story, faltering, was told. Quiet followed. 'That was some spectacular landing you made,' Jake offered.

'Oh, I dunno,' mused Elmer. 'I seen better. But I suppose if you can walk away from it, it was a good landing. Bruce, he's gonna be some kind of mad—first flight for the little sweetheart there, and look how I smashed it up! He's gonna raise some kind of fuss, let me tell you.'

'Oh, fiddle,' Mary Kate told him. 'I'm the one responsible, not you. And Becky, you sent that Mavis person back? That was very brave of you. I'm not sure I could have done that myself. And I thank you, Mr Meadows, for looking after my little chick—to your own hurt, I see.'

'It's nothing, ma'am,' he murmured. 'And besides, I had my own doctor right along with me, didn't I? There was something I wanted to ask you privately, ma'am, if we——'

Whatever it was, it was another of those questions that would have to wait. Jake, having seen his charge to safety, most of it on his iron nerves, wavered, collapsed almost like a jointed tower, and huddled on the ground at their feet.

'Shock,' Becky diagnosed. 'Get that tent up, Elmer. We need to get him warm and sheltered. That's what he needs.'

She bustled around him for half an hour before she was satisfied, and then the three of them—Elmer, Becky, and her mother—gathered around the little fire outside the tent.

'He's sleeping, and the calamity is over, Ma,' Becky laughed. 'Why do you look so darn worried?'

'Well, it's not over,' Mary Kate said sorrowfully. 'The

adventure part is finished, but somebody's got to explain all this to your father. And I have the feeling that I'm elected. Have you got that portable radio set up yet, Elmer?'

'Not quite,' the pilot reported. 'Pretty soon. Don't hardly know as if I got the gumption to turn it on.'

'In a minute,' Mary Kate said. 'First, I have to tell Becky something.'

'Something else wrong?'

Her mother reached over and took her hand. 'Uncle Charlie—he got so excited when you didn't come out on the helicopter, that he—well, he had a heart attack, Becky.'

'Oh, lord, not Uncle Charlie!'

'It was all the excitement, love. And you know Charlie always considered you to be *his* girl.'

'Yes, I know,' Becky sighed. 'He thought that Pop had you and Mattie, and he had nobody; he—he's been a wonderful, loving friend. How is he now?'

'Better, love. He was fighting all the treatments, so I told him I couldn't stand around listening to some old fool complain when I had to go get my Becky out of the woods, and that perked him up right away. I think he'll be okay, what with some rest and recuperation.'

'Oh, heavenly days. Well, that's something I can do for him,' Becky said. 'I'll open up the old farmhouse and we'll sit on the front porch and rock.'

'And go mad,' her mother said very practically. 'Maybe you'd better save me a chair, too. I may need one.'

'What for, Ma?'

'Well, somehow, in all this to-ing and fro-ing, I seem to have forgotten to tell your father.'

'About Uncle Charlie?'

'No, not that exactly, love. I'm afraid—well, Elmer told you, that pile of junk out in the lake was a brand-new plane.'

'That's not important enough to worry about,' Becky returned. 'You could buy him another—or two. What's the *real* problem?' All those years of sharing a home with Mary Kate had left Becky with the healthiest respect for her mother's schemes. 'What exactly is it that you didn't tell Pop?'

'Well—somehow or another, your father told me to go over and see how Uncle Charlie was doing, and I did that, of course. But it seemed to—to slip my mind to tell him I was coming out here after you.'

'Oh, Ma! You didn't!'

'Oh, Rebecca, indeed I did!'

'And you knew he would be worried about your breaking your neck, not his plane? Boy, are you lucky! Some husbands, that would make them so mad they'd really whack you. You're lucky Pop isn't like that.'

'Yes, I am, aren't I?' Mary Kate's voice was just the slightest bit hysterical as she very well remembered once, ten years past, when Bruce Latimore could not have been counted on at all not to whack her bottom. But then, she thought, admittedly she had done a thing or two to aggravate him! Change the subject!

'Tell me about your Mr Meadows, love,' she invited.

Becky leaned over on her mother's shoulder. 'I wish he were,' she whispered. '*My* Mr Meadows, I mean. He's been so wonderful. He saved my life twice. He's been in some terrible pain from those burns and he hasn't complained a bit. He's got a brilliant mind, and strong as—I——'

'That's very nice,' Mary Kate acknowledged, 'but I keep hearing a *but* behind it all. Is he engaged to that Mavis Pell, or something?'

'No. In fact, he doesn't like her too well, and before the fire he was—well, fooling around with me, and——'

'And how much fooling around, Rebecca? I'm not one of those modern who-cares mothers!'

'Nothing—nothing like that, Ma. A little hugging and

kissing, that's all. I *do* remember all the things you taught me!'

'So that's not the problem? Then what is?'

'I don't really know the problem, Ma, just the results. He says I'm a nice girl, and—he just isn't ready for marriage.'

'Oh, my!' Her mother sounded as dejected as Becky did. 'Well, if they won't, they won't. Despite what you read in all the modern novels, there's really no way to trap a perpetual bachelor if he's really got his heart in it. Well, we'll talk later. I think the hour of doom has just caught up to me. Come on, Elmer, turn on the radio and give me the microphone.'

The trip from downtown Boston to Logan Airport had taken Bruce Latimore more time thàn the entire flight across the depth of the state. Consequently, it was seven-twenty-three in the evening when they circled Lenox Mountain and made their initial approach to the Pittsfield airport. Their final destination had been changed when the State Police re-opened the Pittsfield facility to commercial traffic. It was much nearer to Lake Mohawk, and more convenient. Just before they moved into the landing pattern, he waved a hold signal to the pilot, and reached for the company radio for one last report.

'Latimore Control, this is Latimore Six. Over.'

The answer surprised him. As in the military, six was the number assigned personally to him, the chief executive, whether in a car, plane or boat. And every operator knew it. So this particular voice came quickly back, 'Latimore Six, this is Control. Please stand by. We are receiving a weak emergency signal on this frequency.' He took his finger off the microphone switch, and motioned to his own pilot for more altitude, using a thumb as his pointer. Whatever the call was, it was too weak for his aircraft radio to pick it up. The far superior ground system would have to handle the problem. Bruce made a circular motion to his pilot, and they circled the airport at one thousand feet, waiting for developments. They came soon enough. Somewhat over ten minutes later, while he was peering south, searching for smoke and fire from the Beartown Mountain area, the base station returned to him.

'Latimore Six, this is Latimore Control, over.'

'Latimore Six,' he snapped. 'Read you loud and clear. What further trouble?'

'Latimore Six—er—Latimore Six, we have received an emergency message from Latimore Five, by pack radio.'

'By pack radio? Where is that fool woman?'

'Latimore Six—the—there is a message. Shall I read it to you?'

'Yes, damn it!'

'Latimore Six, this is Latimore Control. The complete text of the urgent message is as follows. I quote: "Tell my husband that that fool woman of his has done it again. There are now *four* people at Lake Mohawk who need rescue. Smoke has receded, fire almost extinguished in landing area, there are no immediate medical problems, although the night is getting colder for one injured party". '

'I'll make it a hell of a lot warmer when I get there!' Bruce growled into the microphone.

'Please repeat?' the startled operator stammered.

'If you can make contact again,' he snapped, 'tell my wife that I'm coming at once.'

But Mary Kate Latimore, who knew somewhat more than her family ever gave her credit for, had already turned off the ground radio, and waited patiently for the judgement to come.

It was nine-fifteen of a summer night when two bright stars coasted in gently from the north end of Lake Mohawk, lit up the entire area with the brightest spotlights available for helicopter use, and gradually settled themselves down a little way up the hill from the tiny camp. Mary Kate got up from her seat in the sand, brushed off her dress, and issued her orders.

'Becky, you go inside the tent with your patient. And stay there. Elmer, you go take a long walk along the lake. Keep your eyes open.'

'Sure, Mrs Mary,' he nodded. 'What am I looking for?'

'You're looking to keep your job. Scat!'

So when the two-man medical team came down with the stretcher, she motioned to the tent, and they went quickly and efficiently about their work. When they were a dozen steps up the hill, with Becky walking beside the stretcher, Mary Kate turned around, her hands clenched behind her back. There was her husband, looming over her in the darkness.

'Becky's all right?'

'Yes. But Mr Meadows is hurt, perhaps badly.' Silence. Well, at least he enquired about Becky first, she told herself. Things can't be as bad as I expected.

'Did it again, did you, Mary Kate?'

'I—yes, Bruce. But it's been only twice in ten years, and she's *my* Becky!'

'She's *my* Becky too. Do it again, would you?' She hardly dared to lift her chin, but did anyway.

'Yes.' A firm answer, but very soft, very submissive.

'Come here!'

Bruce pointed to the ground directly in front of him. She squared her shoulders, threw back her head, and walked over.

'I'll pay for the airplane,' she offered hesitantly.

'To hell with the airplane,' he murmured in her ear as he swung her up in his arms. 'It's you I worry about, Mary Kate. Despite what you think, you're not indestructible. Where the hell would I be without you?' She nuzzled her cool cheek against his neck.

'So that's what it's about!' she giggled. 'Pure selfish-

ness. How in the world could you get along without me?'
And then the laughter broke, and the humour disappeared. 'Oh, dear Bruce, I don't want you ever to find out
how you can get along without me. Not ever!'

'And you'll admit she's *my* Becky too?' That stern tone
was back again.

'Of course, love. She always has been—ever since she
and Mattie pushed us into getting married!'

'Damn little vixen,' he chuckled, and then wiped the
grin off his face. 'Both of you, aren't you?'

'If you say so, Bruce.'

He swung her up in the air again and around in a circle
before he dropped her on the ground. She was happy,
excited.

'I do believe you're getting old,' she giggled. 'You
never used to pant like that just from a little exercise!'

'Old!' He was trying to sound stern, but did not quite
get the effect he was looking for. 'I'll show you old, lady.
Just remember your place. Your son Henry already has
four children. That makes you Grandmother Latimore,
doesn't it?'

'Bruce!' she gasped. 'It's all true, but don't you dare say
that out loud! I don't intend to walk down the street at my
age, holding hands with somebody's grandfather!'

'I'll show you *old*,' he threatened. 'Tonight!'

'Well, thank God for that,' she challenged him. They
were both laughing when they ran up the hill.

'Elmer!' Bruce shouted, as he spotted the pilot for the
first time. 'We'll have words, you and I—after you take
two weeks' extra vacation with pay. Hilyard, I want you
all to go back with the medical team in one chopper.
Leave the other one here with me. Becky, is everything
all right with you and your patient?'

She popped out of the big door of the heavy machine
and landed in his arms. 'I didn't dare come out until
you'd finished roaring at Ma,' she laughed.

'Me? Mild-mannered Clark Kent? Roar at your

mother? Never happen,' he chuckled. 'But are *you* all right?' He stripped off his jacket and handed it to her as he spoke.

'Physically I'm fine,' she assured him. 'I lost a little hair. But, Jake—I just don't know. He's pretty badly burned around the shoulder and upper arm, and I love him very much.'

'Well, that's a pretty complex case, doctor,' he chuckled. 'We'll talk about it when we get back. Your mother and I are going to stay for a while, then come back with the second helicopter.'

'Now why in the world would you do that, Pop?'

'None of your darn business, Rebecca Latimore!' He whacked her once on her exposed flank and lifted her back up into the aircraft. 'And for God's sake, put something on—my coat—or something. I won't have my daughter running around half-naked in a plastic raincoat!'

'Maybe I could borrow Ma's blouse,' she shouted down at him. 'From the look of things she won't need it for a while!'

A few minutes later, as they stood hand in hand and watched the loaded chopper take off, Bruce really caught the sense of her farewell. He laughed so hard he had to bend over to relieve the strain on his stomach muscles.

'And just what is all that in honour of?' Mary Kate enquired solicitously.

'That,' he said firmly as he reached out two hungry hands for his wife, 'is what comes of sending a daughter to medical school. She's right—you won't need that blouse at all!'

CHAPTER ELEVEN

IT was an old farmhouse, perched on a hill well back from the county road. It had once been white, and six painters were working full steam to make it so again.

Becky squeezed her father's arm, arguing with him. 'It doesn't have to be all shiny and new, Pop! I don't plan to keep it open for longer than three or four months, until Uncle Charlie can walk around and get his strength back.'

'Becky, girl!' Tall as she was, he had to lean over to tickle her chin with one of his huge fingers. 'It's your house, darling. Just yours. But I was responsible for taking care of it till you needed it. And like a damn fool I've let it run down and go to seed while you were away at school. Now, what kind of a construction man would it make me if I only did a half-proper repair? Besides, Charlie needs a bedroom on the main floor. No more stair-climbing for him for a long time.'

She gave him an enthusiastic hug, and did her best to make her eyes smile to match the rest of her face. But Bruce Latimore was a man who had learned a great deal about women in his ten-year marriage. He knew she was not happy, and would have been willing to bet a dollar or two on the reason. He was also wise enough not to raise the subject. Not directly, that is.

'And when we get him back on his feet, you're off to your surgical residency?' He turned her around and led her down the hill to where the tremendous stump of an old tree stood. And without waiting for an answer to his question, 'Look at that, would you! That's the first place where your mother and I played hanky-panky. Right there!'

166

Her laughter was spontaneous—the first time she had laughed in the eight weeks since they had all returned from Lake Mohawk. But it barely lasted a moment. 'Hanky-panky?' she asked.

'Old-fashioned?' he counter-queried.

'Making out,' she giggled. 'That's what we used to call it. So, you scoundrel, you were making out with my mother on a tree stump?'

'Hah!' he returned. 'Getting your mother alone was a major project in those days. Between you and Mattie haunting us, and Henry looking as if he wanted to push my face in, it was some problem, let me tell you. Wooing is not all that easy a task, lady. Now, about your medical work?'

'I—I don't know, Pop. I sort of feel—what Ma used to say—I've got the dismals. I just don't know. The Corporation isn't going bankrupt, is it?'

'Hardly, love. Michael would never forgive me.'

'Well, then, maybe I'll buy a big rocking chair and a pair of scissors, and just sit on the porch and cut the coupons from my bonds?'

'Well, that'll be some help,' chuckled Bruce. 'At least we'll know where to find *one* of you of a Saturday night!'

'Ma knows everything like that all the time,' Becky returned, and the lilt was back in her voice again. 'Do you know what she said after she cracked up that plane at the lake, before we got things settled?'

'No. What?'

'She said, "Well, I've really done it this time. Maybe you'd better buy three rocking chairs, Becky, and I'll come and join you—just as soon as I can sit down again!" '

'And what do you suppose she meant by that?' he asked cautiously.

'I don't know,' Becky returned. 'Ma doesn't tell us everything, you know.' Her lips were smiling, but Bruce could see the aching vacancy in her eyes.

'Say, that paint's expensive,' he commented. 'I'd

better get back to Boston and make a buck or two more.' He turned her around to face him, and tilted her chin up. 'You don't have anything you want to tell me, love?'

'No, I don't think so, Pop.' He started off down the path to where his car waited, but she stopped him with one hand laid gently on the sleeve of his jacket. 'Ma was pretty lucky,' she said softly. 'I wish I knew where I could find a man like you—I'd chuck all my pills over the wall and marry him in a minute!'

He stopped long enough at the front gate of the family house, in the middle of Eastboro, to talk to Mary Kate. 'You don't have to start holding court until October?'

'That's right. October the sixteenth, in Taunton. That's the plan. But something might come up to upset the whole thing. In any event, we *have* to get things settled before then, Bruce. We just can't sit and watch her drift through life like that. We *have* to do something!'

'Hey, Mary Kate, watch it. I can't think of anything that would make a bigger mess than to have us fiddle around with them.'

'But you're sure it's him?'

'Of course it's him. It's as if she were wearing a big sign on her chest saying, WANTED. DEAD OR ALIVE. JAKE MEADOWS.'

'So where is he, Bruce? At least we could find out that much.'

'And then have a slip of the tongue put her back up? No sirree, Mary Kate. Women are born with tongues, and they mean to wag them.'

'Bruce Latimore, are you talking about me?'

'Not you, love. Lord, I never met a woman who could out-glare or out-silence you—when you put your mind to it. Hey, I gotta run. Be back at six, more or less.'

As he headed the big car up the ramp on to Highway 24 Bruce's fingers doodled on the steering wheel. Should he have told Mary Kate even that much? Somewhere a long time back one of her Irish ancestors must have married a Machiavelli. Mary Kate Latimore was undoubtedly the greatest schemer in all New England. Give her a speck of information, and she could embroider it into a ten-thousand-mile plot. So, certainly, he knew where Jake was.

When the helicopter rescue unit had landed at Logan, it was a military ambulance that waited for Jake. No, he wasn't in the Army any more. Friends at the Pentagon had been quick to reassure him. *But*—he had written a most important book for them, based on his experiences in Vietnam and Lebanon. A most important book.

So a military ambulance had taken him away, and now he was somewhere in Texas, at the military's best burns institute. *Doctor* Jake Meadows, mind you. And wouldn't that shake Becky up if it were sprung on her without any warning! As for how long he might be there, who could tell. And as for what he felt about *my daughter*—well, what father could tell that either! Damn it all, what I ought to do is talk to Mattie about it. Mattie and Becky, just a few years apart, with different fathers and different mothers, and the closest two sisters he had ever seen. He reached for his car telephone, and then drew back. Finding a student at a modern university was like standing on eleven in a blackjack game. It became monotonous, expensive, and highly educational. He picked up his phone and called, instead, his principal secretary, and had her assign three of her brightest young women to the finding of his second daughter.

Despite all the prior planning, it was four o'clock in the afternoon before his secretary buzzed him. 'Your daughter Mathilda is on the phone,' she said, and there was a laugh in her voice.

'Oh, like that, is it,' he chuckled. 'My daughter Mathilda? What the devil have I done wrong now? Put her on, please, Martha. Gently.'

The connections clicked, a couple of tones bonged, and a very determined voice said in his ear, 'So all right, how did you find out so fast that I went out with a communist? It was only last night. And hurry up, I'm at a pay telephone.'

'A communist? Oh, you mean that fellow Ralph something or other. Is he still playing around?'

'Oh, Daddy!' The voice softened. 'He doesn't know the difference between Karl Marx and Groucho Marx. Would you believe it, he was after my money. I thought I'd die when he found out I don't have any! Well, if that isn't the reason, how about calling me back at this number? I've only got eighty-five cents left for the whole week.'

'Okay, okay,' he sighed. 'I don't remember Becky giving me all this trouble, even with all *her* troubles.'

'Becky?' The voice was startled now, concerned. 'What's wrong with Becky?'

'I'll call you back,' he told her. 'Eighty-five cents won't take us through ten per cent of *this* story!'

It took a few minutes to re-establish a connection, and by that time Bruce had had several more thoughts.

'Mattie,' he said quickly, 'I think this is too important to handle on the telephone. You'd better come down here. Grab a cab or something!'

'Or something is right,' she laughed. 'How far do you think you can ride for eighty-five cents in a Boston cab? I can't handle it, Dad.'

'Damn it, girl,' he snapped, 'You've got three million dollars. Why in God's name did you put it into a blind trust? Surely fathers can help their daughters go through college?'

'Did you help Becky?'

'Well—no—you know darn well she wouldn't take the money!'

'And neither will I. I love you lots, Pop, but I'm going to make my life for myself, just like Becky!'

'Damn you two,' he muttered. 'Always the independence! It's all Mary Kate's fault!'

'You bet,' his daughter retorted. 'Now what?'

'Just tell me what street corner you're on, and I'll send a car. And don't you dare argue with me, girl!'

'Woman!' she insisted. 'But don't dilly-dally. This happens to be a corner where a lot of—er—working girls hang around. I wouldn't want to get into the wrong car!'

Half the office staff had gone home before the slim well-curved blonde who was Mattie Latimore bounced into Bruce's office, having waltzed by all the guards and secretaries, and cleared a corner of his desk with an ample hip. 'I must say, you're putting on a little weight,' he snapped, not meaning a bit of it. 'And wearing a dress, too. How about that!'

'I knew you'd be impressed.' Her voice was different from the others in the family. High, clear, happy, it left its mark wherever she went. 'Well?'

'There's nothing *well* about it,' he returned morosely. 'I can't do anything with you, and I can't do anything with Becky. So I thought maybe you could help each other.'

'Becky's in trouble?' The lithe blonde slipped off the desk and plumped herself in a chair. 'Tell me.' He did. It took more than an hour to get it all in.

'And she's—moping around?'

'Not moping, no. She's going ahead madly to get the house ready for Charlie Riley to come to recuperate with her. But there's no fire to her. She's—well, it has to be this man. And he's in Texas.' Which brought on a long discussion about hospitals, burns, and Texas.

'And you don't dare put your foot into the middle of it, Pop? You've got a lot of friends in Texas.'

'Yes,' he groaned, 'and if I made a single move I'd leave footprints on my tongue. No, it's not something I can do.'

'But it is something I can do,' Mattie said very determinedly. 'Nobody treats *my* sister that way. You'd better lend me some quarters. Oh, lord, Texas is a long way off, isn't it? You'd better lend me your telephone credit card.'

Bruce handed over the plastic without an argument. 'I've got to get home,' he said. 'Mary Kate will be worrying her head over this. And there's something funny going on with her, too. Come home for supper with us?'

'Nope,' Mattie returned. 'I'm gonna stay right here and make a few telephone calls.'

The lines between Boston and El Paso, Texas, were extremely busy that night. Mattie had learned a great deal about the army while growing up with her stepsister and stepbrother. So, starting with the night operator at the hospital switchboard, she gradually worked her way up until she arrived at the officer of the day, a brash young man who, in the beginning, lacked two pieces of knowledge. The first being that the Latimore sisters—all of them—were about as persistent as any you might find in the world. The second thing he didn't know—in the beginning—was that Mattie's godfather was Lieutenant-General Alstpastor, a line officer who held medical captains in somewhat less than esteem.

So by ten o'clock that night she was finally connected to a ward nurse. 'I can't do that,' the nurse told her. 'He's a patient, and he's supposed to be asleep.'

'Well,' Mattie lied very effectively, 'I'm sorry. I'm sure he's awake—he never sleeps. And it's a case of a possible death in the family!'

'Okay, I give up,' the nurse sighed. 'I'll go see.'

In another five minutes there was a click on the line, and a deep bass voice said, 'Meadows. What the hell is this? My family don't know I'm here.'

Before he could hang up she caught his attention. 'A lot you know,' she said bitterly. 'My name is Mattie Latimore. Becky is my sister.'

'Oh, lord,' he exclaimed. 'Becky? They told me she wasn't injured at all. She's dying?'

'The question, Mr Meadows, is how much longer you mean to hang around down there getting your back healed?'

'Lord, that's been over for two or three weeks. They've got me tied down to finish this stupid book!'

'And you're the only one who can write the book?'

'Well, I'd say I'm the only one who can put it together. If I had a couple of secretaries, or something, I suppose I could do it in my spare time.'

'How long would it take with two secretaries and a mainframe IBM computer?' she asked.

'You've got that kind of influence?'

'I've got it. How soon can you leave? Tomorrow morning?'

'Why wait that long?' he grunted. 'Not if Becky is— I'm putting my damn pants on now. Why tomorrow morning?'

'Because that's the soonest I can get a jet down there to pick you up.'

'To hell with that,' Jake growled. 'I've got plenty of jet jockeys down here who owe me a favour. Where *is* Becky?'

'At the farmhouse. There seemed to be no use keeping her in hospital, so they brought her home.'

'Oh, my God! Look, I'll have to fly into a military airport.'

'How about Bedford?' she suggested. 'Lincoln Laboratory. I think they still have a runway open. What time can you make it?'

He mused for a moment or two. 'I can't tell,' he returned. 'Early morning. How will I recognise you?'

'Easy,' she laughed. 'I'll be the only blonde asleep in my father's Mercedes. Is that all?'

'No,' he said soberly. 'I've met most of your family— and wondered on occasion whether they had all their marbles. Is this on the up and up? Does Becky know I'm coming?'

'No,' Mattie responded to the first comment. 'There's not a word of truth in it. The rest of them are all nice people. I'm the devious one.'

'Take after your mother, do you? What's wrong with Becky?'

'Yes, I *do* take after Ma, and no, Becky doesn't know you're coming, and I don't *know* what's wrong with her. She sits down on that tree-stump and watches people paint her house, and she wouldn't care if the world stopped so she could step off.'

'And you don't like that?'

'Of course I don't like that. She's my sister! I love her a lot. When I was just a litle mixed-up kid, Becky shared her mother with me. You can't ask for a bigger gift than that!'

'Funny thing,' Jake returned, 'I can remember her saying the same thing about you—that she loved you because you shared your father with her. But where does that get me? I love your sister very much myself, but I didn't get a great deal of encouragement, you know. She told me that a lot of girls might fall in love with me easily, but not her.'

'I'll bet that isn't an exact quote.'

'Well—maybe not, come to think of it. But she could have said, couldn't she?'

'And you could have said. Did you?'

'Hell, no. Who wants to come out in the open like that, and then get turned down?'

'Then why do you suppose Becky wouldn't feel the same way?'

'You mean to tell me I've been a stupid jackass all this time?'

'You won't be the first one in our family—er—Jake?'

'Yeah, Mattie. You'd better hang up before you owe the telephone company your life. Anything else?'

'Just one more thing, Jake. My brother Henry is a very big man, and I've got two Harvard football players on my string. If you come up here and hurt Becky, I'll go out of my way to arrange a private stomping party for you. Got the message?'

'Wow! I heard you. If I come up there and hurt Becky again I'll lie down quietly so you can stomp away. The blonde sleeping in the Mercedes, huh? I'll see you some time after dawn.'

It was hard to keep a secret in the Latimore family for as long a time as four days. Which was the time it took for Jake to finish his book, for Mary Kate to surprise the family, and for Bruce to come to admire the man.

'Burst right into my office,' he told Mary Kate. 'Said he'd come to marry my daughter, and what the hell objections did I have.'

'And you told him some,' Mary Kate laughed.

'Not me,' Bruce returned. 'For four days I haven't had a secretary, and nobody could use the computer, and there were papers and people all over the place. So I told him that if he planned to elope with her, I'd come and hold the ladder.'

'You what! Bruce Latimore, you——'

'And that's what I told him, too,' the big man laughed. 'I told him that I didn't mind, but her mother would kill him if there wasn't a church wedding, and all that. And that's the last I saw of him. Nice man.'

Michael ran through the living room at that point, heard the last words, and whooped. 'Nice man coming? Nice man?'

'Yes, dear,' Mary Kate laughed. 'And on your birthday, too. Four years old, Michael. That many!' She held up four fingers and the boy emulated her.

'I've got to do some work,' his father chuckled. 'You set your scheme in motion, and——'

'Mattie's scheme,' Mary Kate insisted. 'Mattie's.'

'Okay, set Mattie's scheme in motion. I'll hide in the library until my blessings are required.'

'Typical male,' his wife snorted, 'always leaving the dirty work to the women!'

Becky was up early that day, as usual. It was something bred into her by farm life. She managed a cup of instant coffee, shuffled herself into a pair of tired denims, an old sweater, and a scarf to tie over her hair. They had re-styled it for her, but it was not even close to what it had been. She sauntered down the path to the old tree-stump, all that was left of the Eastboro Liberty Tree.

The painters came early, just after eight o'clock, set up their ladders, and began to work. The size of the bonus offered by Mr Latimore had inspired them to all sorts of unexpected effort.

At eight-thirty Anna came up from the other house, down around the side of the hill, where she, Henry, and their four children operated a dairy farm. It was a surprise to Becky. Anna, a towering Scandinavian girl, was a bundle of fun, but at this time of morning was usually tied up with getting her husband off to work, her children off to school, and her dishes done—just in case her tiny mother-in-law came by to inspect. She was in her seventh month, and moving was somewhat difficult. She puffed up to where Becky sat and found herself a space on the capacious stump. 'Warm, huh?'

'Yeah. For September,' Becky returned softly. 'Kids okay?'

'Oh *jah*, all good.'

'Henry?'

'As usual, he works. The painters, you get them to come early. They must like you.'

'Come on, Anna, you know darn well Pop slipped them something under the table. I don't know who he thinks he's fooling!'

Anna settled more comfortably and watched. 'You hear the family news last night?'

'Family news?' Becky shook herself. No, she hadn't

heard the family news. She had been too deep in her own fit of depression to contact the family in almost a week, and strangely enough, until this moment, none of them had come over to see her!

'Well,' Anna laughed, 'Ma has resigned from the bench. She notified the Governor yesterday.'

'What! Why in the world would she do that?'

'She's pregnant! Pop says it's that Bermuda water. Ma says it comes from hanging around in helicopters at Lake Mohawk!'

'But the doctor said——'

'Ah!' Anna threw up her hands. 'Doctors? What do they know! Oh, excuse me, Becky.'

'I can hardly believe it,' Becky sighed. 'She's—not too young, Anna.'

'Only thirty-nine. Hey, look at your painters!'

Becky had been watching them all this time. In the distance she could hear her telephone ring. One of the men working on the window moulding waved and went in. When he came out again, all the painters stopped work. Then, faster than they had put them up, the ladders came down, were loaded on a pair of trucks parked in front of the house, and everybody climbed in. As the truck passed the tree-stump, the foreman leaned out. 'Be back tomorrow, Becky!' he shouted. She barely heard the 'maybe' that went with it.

Anna watched them go down off the hill, around the curve, and out of sight. She found her way ponderously to her feet. 'Got to get Henry's lunch,' she announced. 'Nice to talk to you, Becky. See you after a while.'

And just what the devil does that mean? Becky asked herself suspiciously. I love Anna, but we haven't exchanged twenty words in two weeks. Nice to talk to you, Becky? Something's fishy here.

It had grown quiet. Why not, she thought—there's nothing going on. And there won't be, for all the endless years. She stared up at the house again. It was almost finished. Uncle Charlie would be pleased. He was coming down by ambulance on Monday, and then— what a lonely time it would be. Where could Jake be? That was the part that hurt. Not a word, not even a postcard. Off with Mavis Pell, maybe?

That idea gave her a little sting of remorse. She had actually hired a clipping bureau—one of those offices that read all the papers and cut out references to specific people—with instructions to follow Mavis Pell. In five weeks she had received a load of clippings from the Albany papers, but not a single entry about Jake. She rubbed hard at her eyes with rough knuckles. No tears, Doctor Latimore. That's for kids.

The sun was warming things up. She turned her back to welcome it. Behind her, down on the county road, a car stopped, a door banged, and the car went on. She started to turn her head, then stopped. Why bother?

Steps on the gravel path startled her. She almost turned around again. Almost—she could feel the hair on the back of her neck stand up. Something electrical, behind her, and she dare not turn around. She dare not, for her life.

Her hands ran up under the scarf, smoothing what was left of her raven-black hair. She pulled the scarf tighter over it. The footsteps came closer, hesitated, stopped.

'Becky?' *His* voice, deep, patterned, controlled. She clamped a rigid control on her nerves, and slowly turned to look over her shoulder.

'Why, it's Jake Meadows!' Come to break the rest of my heart have you, Jake? She patted the stump beside her.

'Sit down, Jake.' That's the way. A neutral tone. You tell *me* something before I'll tell you! She felt the warmth of his hip against hers.

'I've missed you, Becky.'

'Have you really? I didn't notice any letters or phone calls or visits or anything!' Sarcasm. Drive it home. After all, I've got some pride left, and if he really doesn't want me, I don't want to hear him *say* it. Lord, wouldn't that be the ever-loving end!

'It's pretty hard to visit all the way from a Texas hospital, Becky.' Quietly said, with no emotion showing.

She was up and around in an astoundingly fluid movement. 'In the hospital, Jake? Oh, God! And I never knew!' She stuffed both hands into her mouth to cut off the sobs. This is no way to be nonchalant, she yelled at herself. He reached up and gently pulled her down again, closer than before. 'What have you been doing these last weeks, Becky?'

Dying for want of you, she wanted to scream, but of course could not. 'I—well, there's Uncle Charlie, you might remember. He had a heart attack, and I thought—well, I have this house. This is my house, Jake, and I thought I would fix it up and Uncle Charlie could recuperate here for a couple of months because he's a bachelor, you know, and .. .' Stop! she commanded herself. You're babbling—running off at the mouth like some fool co-ed. Shut up!

'And then back to the surgery. Have you established your residency?'

'I—no—no. I—I've changed my mind, Jake. When Uncle Charlie is in good enough shape, I thought I would find some little hospital, and—and—I thought I would go into paediatrics, not surgery.'

'You like kids?'

'Yes, I—do you?'

'Yes, I like kids. My own.'

'You—I didn't think you had any kids, Jake.'

'I don't,' he laughed. 'Not yet. I just like kids.' There was a moment of silence, both of them inspecting the house as if it were in a strange land.

'Your arm, Jake? Was it terribly infected from the burns?'

'Oh, it wasn't really anything. Take a look.' He slipped

off his sweater and laid his bare arm over her shoulder. She shivered, but not from the cold. The scar tissue glared at her, and she stroked it gently, teasing it with soft firm fingers. Without thinking, she held the arm in both her hands, and kissed the scars at the inside of the elbow.

'Good job,' she murmured. 'Was that at the Army burns centre?'

'Yes.' He made no move to take his arm away, and just in case the idea should cross his mind, she clung to it with both hands. He moved a little closer, warming her against the late September breeze.

'Your house,' he gestured. 'It's important to you? The only place you could live?'

Becky turned a flustered face up to him. 'The house? Lord, I'm not house-proud, Jake! It's where I was born, and where Ma and I lived when Pop came along and married all of us. All this——' she waved her hand in a wide arc '—all this was left to Henry and me. Henry's my real brother, you know. He's the farmer. He lives down there. You can just see the tip of his roof.'

'And?'

'And Henry likes to be a farmer, and he's married to Anna, and she likes to be a farmer's wife, and they've got four children, and that's what you need to run a farm these days. So I thought—when Uncle Charlie and I were through with the farmhouse, I'd give the whole thing to Henry—because Henry's not a Latimore, you see. He's a Chase. I was a Chase, too, but when Ma married, Pop adopted me and that's why I'm a Latimore, you see.' She had to stop. She had run out of breath, and there was a curious feeling playing up and down her spine.

'Yes, I can see,' he said solemnly. 'But it's a funny thing. When I talk to you Latimores I get a lot of wonderful words, but no answers.'

'I didn't answer you? I—Jake—I'm afraid I've forgotten the question.'

'The question was, are you so tied up in this house now that you couldn't live anywhere else?' Before she could form an answer, both of his arms landed around her waist, lifted her up, and plumped her down again so that she was facing him squarely. 'Now then, the answer,' he chuckled. She started to turn her head away, but he caught her chin. 'No, you don't! I want some straight answers, and I want to see your eyes while you make them,' he growled.

'I—I don't understand what you mean, Jake. I—yes—I—no, of course not. I could live most anyplace. Anyplace—I—does that answer the question?'

'That answers *one* of them. Now, next. I seem to remember when we were dodging fireballs up at that lake, that you made a statement about how easy it would be for a girl to fall in love with a man like me. And then you said "present company excepted, of course". Now just what did that mean?'

'It's—just what you say when—when you mean it to be a hypothetical statement. Not anybody directly concerned, or—or—I don't know why I said such a stupid thing—why am I crying?'

'It'll do you good to cry a little,' Jake said quietly. Becky leaned against him, resting her head on his chest. She could feel him touching her scarf, and moved away. 'No, please, don't touch that,' she sniffled.

'So-o!' He unwound the scarf and tossed it aside. 'There's a lot of girl inside the doctor, isn't there?'

'It's a terrible mess,' she muttered. 'I wanted it to be all regrown when—if . . .'

'It will grow back,' he reassured her.

'How do you know?' she growled at him. 'How the devil do you know that it won't be all fuzzy and spots for the rest of my life? What was I doing before you got so nasty?'

'You were crying on my shirt,' he answered softly. 'Try it again. It'll do you a lot of good.' She didn't want to resist. His strong hands gathered gently around her, and brought her head back against his chest. The tears seemed to follow as if preordained. 'That's better,' he whispered.

'What are you doing?' she demanded through the tears.

'I'm kissing your ear. The left one,' he said. 'When I get through with that I'm going to kiss the right one. And when you're tired of crying, and I'm tired of kissing ears, I have a present for you.'

'Not yet,' she sighed. 'I'm not ready yet.' She coiled up against him, putting both arms around his waist. Well, almost three-quarters of the way. Five minutes passed. He heard a rustling in the bush behind them, and moved slightly away from her. His movement startled her. She drew back and wiped her eyes on her sleeve. 'I didn't bring a handkerchief,' she sighed. 'My mother brought me up to be a lady, and I forget. What was the present you brought me?'

'Aha!' he chuckled. 'Fell into the old trap, did you? Always bring them a present. I learned that when I was a baby!'

Becky banged her hand down on the stump. It hurt. 'Why, you—you must have been a terrible little boy,' she snapped.

'Terrible,' he agreed. 'I hope to have all girls. I understand they're easier to raise than boys. Want your present now?'

'Of course I do, Jake Meadows,' she sighed. He reached into the heavy pocket of his jeans and brought out a wrapped package. She tore at the paper, paying no attention to the long hours that Mary Kate had drilled her: 'People who bring presents have wrapped them with love. You should unwrap them slowly.' And then she saw the contents. A book!

To be truthful, not exactly a book yet, but a typed manuscript. Her eyes were distorted still by tears. She read the first page. There was a title, and a printed dedication. 'To Doctor Rebecca Latimore, for her research assistance, and her tolerance.'

She shook her head to get the tears out of her eyes. 'What a life this is going to be!' Jake chuckled as he handed her a handkerchief. She managed to clear her eyes, turned to the next page and looked at the title.

'*EMERGENCY PROCEDURES FOR FIELD SURGERY*,' it said. Published and approved by the Department of Defense. By Brigadier General Jake R Meadows, MD, Chief of Field Surgery, US Army.

'Why—why, that's you, Jake!' she exclaimed, astonished.

'I believe so,' he chuckled. 'That's what I was finishing up at the cabin. And when it's printed you'll have one of the first copies.'

'And you're a surgeon—and a general? A real general?'

'No, not any more,' he said. 'I retired—from being a general, I mean, not from being a surgeon. This book is my final contribution.'

'Well!' she sighed deeply, and nestled closer to him. 'I'm glad you're retired. Uncle Charlie was a sergeant in the Second World War, and he thinks all generals are meatheads. And a surgeon, too. You must think me a fool!'

Jake tapped her nose with one finger. 'Don't be putting words in my mouth,' he said quietly. 'I think you're a lot of things, but *fool* is not one of them.' He pulled her close again.

'Is that all the questions?' she asked.

'My, how humble!' he returned. 'Nope. I've got a couple more whenever you're ready.'

'Yes, I'm ready. Fire away—I mean, go ahead.'

'Once you told me you were so rich you didn't have to work at all. Is that true?'

'Well, yes and no,' she sighed. 'I suppose I have a great

deal of money, but it's all in a blind trust. Once a year the trustees meet, select the most needy charity they can find, and they give all the profits away.'

'And then another year's worth accumulates?'

'Yes. It comes from my shares in the Corporation. Pop likes to work. Whenever he works, he makes a lot of money. And then we—Ma and Mattie and I—we give it away. It's Mary Kate's idea. She says keeping him working keeps him young, and she has a special fund that she's saving for their retirement. It sounded so good that Mattie and I both did the same thing. Is that the right answer?'

'That's the right answer, lady. Come a little closer.' Jake had put on his wool sweater again. She slid as close as she could, drying her eyes on his sweater. 'So you wouldn't mind marrying a man and living on his *small* income?'

'I wouldn't mind,' she sniffled. 'That is, if it's——' and she hadn't the nerve to say, in case it might be unlucky!

'You know something?' she substituted. 'When Ma and Pop were courting, there were so many people in the house that they had to sneak down here to the Liberty Tree to make out.'

'To make out? I'm not up on some of these phrases. What does it mean?'

Becky snuggled sideways against him, lifted one of his hands, and cuddled it against her breast. She could hear his breath whistle in a surprised hiss. Gradually his fingers closed, gently but firmly. 'Like that?' he whispered.

'Like that,' she returned.

His hand moved down to the waistband of her blouse, slipped beneath it, and gradually slid up the smooth softness of her skin to try the match again. She hardly ever wore a bra, so interference was minimal. The quivering fortress surrendered without a shot as Jake's fingers surrounded its bronze tip and snapped it to

attention. Becky shuddered deliciously. 'If there's another question, ask it quickly,' she pleaded.

'Lord, yes,' he sighed. 'You've got two of these. You'll
drive me crazy! Your parents came here for privacy?'

'Yes,' she giggled, 'but we don't have to worry about
things like that.'

'We don't?' he chuckled. 'We're already surrounded!'
He drew his hand out from under her blouse. 'Do you
suppose your father would agree to your marrying me?'

'Faith! Faith Latimore!' The call came from the
farmhouse down the hill, and it was obvious that Anna
Chase was angry. 'Faith Latimore, you spying little
monster! Come back here!'

Jake didn't look around, but did talk over his shoulder.
'Am I doing all right, Faith?'

The little girl stood up, brushed the debris from her
slacks, and walked around in front of them. 'You could
have done better,' she sighed, 'but Becky's a hard one to
get going. Don't worry about Pop. This morning he was
all upset over his breakfast. "If he don't marry her
quickly, I think I'll shoot him!" he yelled at Ma. "How
long can you expect a normal fellow like me to live in the
middle of all this confusion?"'

'And what did your mother say?'

'She just laughed and said, "Don't forget you've got
three more daughters to go, Grandfather!"'

'Hey, that sounds hopeful,' chuckled Jake. 'One more
thing, Becky. There's a little hospital down in Middle-
boro. Saint Luke's, it's called. Nice place. They could use
a practising couple in a few months, after Uncle Charlie
is better.'

'Sounds good to me,' Becky returned. Her face was
blush-red, her head down, and one of her feet was
swinging nervously back and forth.

'So what the heck have I forgotten now?' he
complained.

'You're supposed to kiss her and ask her to marry you,'

snapped Faith. 'At this rate you'll both be over forty before I can get you to the altar!'

'Don't count on it, kid,' he laughed. 'I know all about that part. Now you get home—pronto!' Without waiting for compliance he swept Becky up in his arms and stalked up the hill towards the house.

'There surely must be someplace around here where a fellow can get some privacy!' he snorted, as he slammed the screen door behind him.

'Maybe,' she laughed, snuggling closer. 'It all depends on what you have in mind. Whatever it is, you'd better hurry. Today is Michael's fourth birthday, and the whole family is coming to celebrate it here at eleven o'clock. That's two hours from now.'

'That's enough time,' growled Jake. 'And to show you what a sport I am, I'll stay for the party, too. Would you like that?'

'I'd like anything you want to do,' she sighed. 'But couldn't you hurry a little faster?'

ATTRACTIVE, SPACE SAVING BOOK RACK

Display your most prized novels on this handsome and sturdy book rack. The hand-rubbed walnut finish will blend into your library decor with quiet elegance, providing a practical organizer for your favorite hard-or soft-covered books.

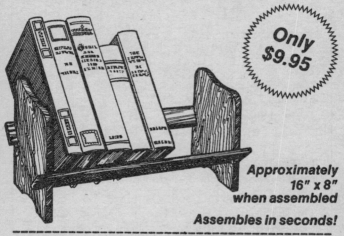

Only $9.95

Approximately 16" x 8" when assembled

Assembles in seconds!

HMV·B·1

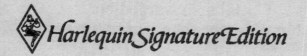

Harlequin Signature Edition

Carole Mortimer

Merlyn's Magic

She came to him from out of the storm and was drawn into his yearning arms—the tempestuous night held a magic all its own.

You've enjoyed Carole Mortimer's Harlequin Presents stories, and her previous bestseller, *Gypsy*.

Now, don't miss her latest, most exciting bestseller, *Merlyn's Magic*!

IN JULY

MERMG

Take 4 best-selling love stories FREE
Plus get a FREE surprise gift!